TRUE FICTION

TRUE FICTION

short stories by
Sohrab Homi Fracis

STEPHEN F. AUSTIN STATE UNIVERSITY PRESS

For more information:
Stephen F. Austin State University Press
P.O. Box 13007 SFA Station
Nacogdoches, Texas 75962
sfapress@sfasu.edu
www.sfasu.edu/sfapress

Managing Editor: Kimberly Verhines
Book design: Katt Noble

Distributed by Texas A&M Consortium
www.tamupress.com

ISBN: 978-1-62288-932-7

CONTENTS

Open Mic

A DARK-HAIRED WHITE GIRL WITH TATTOOS and piercings raps "Move, Bitch" like she's black. Except she doesn't say the N-word, so that throws her rhythm off. We clap along anyway. Along the near-corridor that is Five Points Coffee & Spice, the bittersweet aroma of roasted Arabica mingles with the Thai tang of Sriracha Buffalo Wings. The young woman by the back room shifts her hips as she nears the end of her rap and skips an F-word. Not the fucks—she hits those and the B-word with urgency: "Get out the way, bitch, get out the way." No, it's the old slur for gay. A decade has passed since Ludacris wrote the song. There's a brother in the White House, and some of us are still pinching ourselves.

The next guy up on Open Mic shuffles things around, hooking the amp to his acoustic guitar. Its wood gleams and a painted feather sticks out from under its keys. He's a scruffy-bearded young regular by the name of Max. Longish light hair falls across his forehead to screen his most distinctive feature: a permanently closed eye. In his black tee over jeans he could be the badass hipster, but he's on the tubby side and when he speaks he mumbles and stammers. He doesn't do vocals, just blues and folk-rock progressions that are uneven and not easily identifiable. Still, the guitar has a warm tone and the progressions are ambitious, incorporating bass lines behind the chords and lead riffs above them. All a bit rough, but everyone likes the soft-spoken youngster and we applaud in anticipation of his mute acknowledgment.

The customer in charge of today's signup sheet has to go look for the next performer, who has probably stepped out onto Lomax for a smoke. Approaching the entrance, he stops in his tracks to stare up at a figure that has to stoop through. It's the only seven-footer any of us is likely to run into. Surreal and somehow heartening to see Henri's shoulders float above the heads of other customers as he moves through them, smiling and nodding, toward the other brown face in the room.

"Pervez," he says in his thick voice, dropping a huge hand on my shoulder. I'm decades older than him and not far short of six feet, but I feel like a child angling its face upward. "How are you?"

"Hey, Henri." I lift my voice, too, against the buzz. "What's happening?"

Looking eager and happy to tell me, he launches into a detailed account. His expressiveness is magnetic, and as always I lean in attentively. But, as always, I'm unable to decipher every fifth word, which is often mangled or a substitute that doesn't make sense. I can't follow the logic of first his longer sentences and then the entire thread. I can tell it's clear in his head, yet what's pouring out of his mouth is a fascinating jumble that I cannot recreate. Before long I'm listening for key words and phrases to which to nod and make vaguely comprehending noises. My ability to converse in French, let alone Kinyarwanda, is nonexistent, so I admire Henri for his courage in English.

Courage in general. I've never asked whether he's Tutsi or Hutu, but I have gathered that his family came to the States by way of Burundi under some form of political asylum. They spoke no English. They could carry little. In Rwanda he was an apprentice accountant; here he's a Wendy's cashier. His journey out into the world must feel like in some ways he's going backward.

Direction is a topic on many a night here: specifically, what the future might hold. Not only for each of us but for Five Points and the coffee shop. We're a varied clientele—students, veterans, cyclists, bikers, cops, artists, cops who are artists, techies, stand-up comedians, techies who are stand-ups, even a resident magician—but there's a general fear of gentrification. Rumors abound of landlords ratcheting up rents, following the great recession, to push out grungy hipster hangouts and make room for more upscale or yuppie establishments. The shop's owner Alva, sporting a yellowish goatee and elongated earlobes, says people should support a local independent business over a national franchise like Starbucks. I live in the new apartments across from Starbucks, which makes me a part of the gentrification. When convenience takes me there, I feel like a traitor. Cozy Tea, a British Indian place in Five Points, closes at four, so at least I don't have to choose between local and global. It's both, when you think about it. Like me. Like Henri.

Seen from the inside, Five Points Coffee & Spice could be a closed system, independent of and impervious to external forces. Nothing much changes, or so it seems. Max plays Open Mic after Open Mic. Not just solo. He accompanies singers on his feathered guitar and sits in on group performances. But he never sings, and barely says a word. Occasionally a loose-limbed giant with a slight limp obscures my line of vision, Henri pours his latest into my attentive ear, and I fail to follow. Undaunted, he rambles on.

ON A FIRST FRIDAY ONE MONTH, we're all packed a little tighter. Five Points celebrates the start of the month in streets lined with buskers, their guitar cases open for tips. Folk and bluegrass trios harmonize at the corners. A whiff of weed drifts across the entrance to Lomax Lodge, out of which heavy metal roars. Inside the coffee shop, Open Mic has hit a boisterous Irish vein. A guitarist with a beret and a Gaelic-sounding name like Colin or Conan or Conner announces an original and shouts its refrain: "Fuck the British!" Presumably inspired, Katie, a regular who narrowly clears the little-person bar, sings her own original and gets us to join in on a two-word chorus: "Guys suck!"

Max comes on, multicolored wrist-bands on both arms, and settles into an extended blues improvisation. The quiet change-up allows talk to resume. The LARPers or Live Action Role Players in medieval costumes are buzzing about something. Eventually the cyclists stop cussing the city for its biking infrastructure or lack of much and tune in to the LARPers. Mouths open wide, hands go to the sides of heads. I'm thinking Max sounds pretty good tonight, like all his playing is starting to pay off, when cries of dismay counterpoint some nifty chord progressions.

Max trails off, confused, his one open eye startled. "What's going on?" he says into the mic. Like the 4 Non Blondes, except he doesn't shout it. More like a Marvin Gaye "What's Going On." Max may never have shouted a question in his life. The people who answer him without a mic sound louder. And unsettled. The LARPers have been told they will not be able to meet here next month. It's official: our refuge from the world, which has prided itself on staying open to 3 a.m. night after night, year after year, will shut down forever. There's no such thing as a perfect closed system, unless it's the universe. Even that is a maybe.

My cappuccino cools off as I fight a sense of disorientation. Looking around, I spot a beautiful, close-cropped, warrior head a foot above the rest being shaken in disbelief. Instinctively I drift toward Henri. He looms like some central fount of life, like a huge queen bee from whom all the swarming bees in the hive are descended.

"Hey, Henri," I say, throwing my palms apart. "No more Coffee & Spice."

"Pervez." Shoulders at my eye level shrug. "Crazy, man. This is my new home. You know? Now my *new* home is gone."

"I know, man. I think we're all feeling like that."

At a nearby table, our resident magician who is a Desert Storm veteran artfully reveals the right card to a pretty young woman. She puts her hands to her face and exclaims in astonishment. As if realizing this may be his last bit of magic in here, the unshaven vet flips his marked pack over to show her the patterns.

"So what have you been up to?" I say.

Henri nods. "I play a lot of football. It is my team—I start it. I am the goalie, you know." He spreads his arms, his fingertips just short of the counter and the rough brick wall covered in artwork. Hard to imagine the ball getting past that wingspan. "It is not as good as in Kigali, because my leg is injured." He limps to demonstrate. "My doctor tell me it will be better, but I must be careful." He grins. "I don't tell him I play football. I am not a forward, running on the field. You know? I tell him I study very hard for my license. Then one day I tell my boss his job is not good for me. I am an accountant, Pervez. You know? One day he will come to me for his accounts."

"Awesome." My mood lifts.

But there's something going on that, in all the confusion, I can't pin down. I look at Henri, and do a double take. He has that head laid back, watching me with a slight smile that blends mischief and anticipation. And suddenly my head is tingling, my eyes are bulging, my mouth is opening, and I'm shouting above the hubbub: "Henri! I can follow everything you're saying! Every bit of your English makes sense now! Every single word!"

The smile goes wide. His nod is cocky. He flourishes an acknowledgment. "This is one more language, Pervez. I have many."

"Sure. But you're too old to just sponge it up like kids can. You still went at it and for years you just let your tongue go, no matter how it came out. No fear!"

He's sober now, head laid back again, eyes dark, appraising me. "It is not a thing to fear. It is only hearing, talking, hearing, talking. Talking small things. You know? But what I see in Kigali...I don't talk. Those things I will never talk."

Unspeakable things float in the depths of those eyes, and I don't ask.

People around us start to spill out into the street. It's time for the fire show on First Fridays. Lomax is blocked off and the occasional car sent around it, honking. The torches take a while to light in the October night chill. Then they burn fiercely, and the performers swing them in great fiery circles through the dark. They march back and forth, as Alva the ringmaster cracks a bullwhip thrice his body-length. Eventually the circles of fire dim for the last time. Five Points Coffee & Spice has flamed out.

LOMAX LODGE CLOSES TOO—no more head-banging shows. So does Underbelly, whose open-air stage under trees and night sky was never a closed system. Reportedly, the residents of Riverside Presbyterian invoked the noise ordinance. It feels like Five Points' version of the day the music died.

Yet nowadays there's a digital kind of immortality to be had. A year later on Facebook, I see a post to the old coffee shop's page. Someone has just rated it 5 stars along with the comment "*Still* better than Starbucks." I go to the page and "like" it. Scrolling down the posted pics and videos is like going down memory lane. Alva and his crew still pour steaming espressos and serve up hot wings. The artwork is still on the walls. Max still cradles his feathered acoustic. Open Mic still rocks. The LARPers still swagger and vamp their way in and out the back room. The hipsters still have their beloved hangout.

Then I hit a post that makes me swallow. It's a memorial announcement for Max. His second eye, too, has closed forever. No one knows how or why. An outpouring of comments, some addressing him as if he's still there, expresses love and grief for the gentle young man.

I add mine belatedly and return to the video in which I'd seen him still alive. It records the day the shop's OPEN sign went out for good. Regulars and staff speak of what it means to them and how much it will be missed. One of them tears up and can't continue. Max is the only one featured who says nothing. He just plays his guitar.

Behind the opening montage, a lush finger-picking pattern descends in a minor key. There's something of the guitarist's melancholy sweetness in the cascading notes. When his fingers appear along the fretboard, they move nimbly and the painted yellow feather signals undeniable flair. I hear resonance with an old Led Zeppelin standard, "Going to California." Robert Plant's eerily high voice begins to play in my head: "I think I might be sinking."

I kick up the volume on my laptop, and Max plays on. He sounds really good.

All Right, Now, Cupid

My self-summary
Taking a turn onto Stockton last month, I saw a pedestrian stumble up onto the curb, almost into the path of my Sonata, and stagger back onto the sidewalk. He was a blind man with a long folding cane, and on his own. His shirt was tucked, unusual in our increasingly hipster neighborhood. Alarmed by his misstep, he swept the path frantically with his cane as he lurched ahead through his personal minefield. It broke my heart.

I was on my way to Bold Bean, but I felt my coffee could wait. Looking for a spot to pull over, I noticed a woman walking the other way—out for a stroll through Riverside, taking the air on a sunny day in a below-the-knees skirt. Slowing up at the light, I turned to see her go straight up to the blind man and put a hand to his arm.

He jumped back at first. I've tried to imagine what life would be like if I were blind, even gone about my chores with an eye-patch on. But it's impossible to know. Can't say if blind faith would come easier to him or harder. I have friends who are atheist—I'm agnostic myself, happy to believe in the incredible yet credible universe.

I felt that the universe had brought her to him. As the light turned, I saw her take his cane hand in hers, stilling his jumpy moves and speaking to him quietly. I caught the look on his face as he listened. It was a beautiful thing.

What I'm doing with my life
I know, that wasn't exactly a self-summary. But what would a literal one leave for these other spaces?

So: what I'm doing with my life.

I don't even know what I'm doing on OkCupid. I'm retired. From a downtown bank, a year ago, and glad of it. You wouldn't believe the politics at our Jacksonville branch. A teller caught in the middle was fired and went postal. You might remember it from the news. If not, I've got the inside story: see *The Six Things I Could Never Do Without*. It's my Charles Bukowski story. Did you know his postman character, Chinaski, was really him? That's my kind of fiction. What's the point if it's all just made up? Chinaski's something of an ass, but still. Consider this an advance entry for *Favorite Books*.

I'm really good at
...not doing things when I'm expected to.

It's part of why I never married. I understood why women wanted that, but I knew a couple who were great friends for a while, then did well enough in a relationship, then split within a year of getting married, then hated each other through the divorce, then became friends again once the exponentially increasing expectations they'd heaped on each other finally fell off their shoulders with a thud.

At this stage of our lives, though, I imagine women have less need of marriage. The window for raising a family has shut. It's just about us now.

The first things people usually notice about me
They don't usually. Notice me. When Ralph Ellison wrote, "I am invisible, understand, simply because people refuse to see me," he might as easily have been speaking of a retiree as a black man back in the '40s.

You know what I'm talking about. My accurately stated age (unlike a few on the site) didn't stop you—even though retired is as good as dead, online—nor did my weathered face, my balding head, or my talk of old-fashioned folk in tucked shirts and longer skirts. You must know what it is to have aged in a young people's world, maybe even a youthful neighborhood.

I've heard it hits women earlier, not long after the bloom is off the rose. Comes as a shock that they've no longer got it and men aren't all over them anymore. The male gaze suddenly ignores them. And funny thing: they miss it.

But now, online, middle-aged women find they still have it: backlit by the screen, glowing, in demand again, approached not just by a handful but a hundred lonely men. So it's hard for men to be noticed in the crowd of thumbnail pics and messages left unread. On the other hand when *you* message us, it's an occasion. We notice.

If you've got your bloom back, you probably have no need of me, and I hope the right guy's in the pile. But then why would you be searching profiles; why are you reading mine? No, if you're here, you're either past that second blossoming or you don't care for the crowd.

Favorite books, movies, shows, music, and food
Well, neither *Invisible Man* nor *Birdman.*

The hero I want is Retiredman. And/or Retiredwoman. Cue a softer, melodic theme, not *Birdman*'s driving drumbeat. Michael Keaton is still too engaged, too vigorous, too straight-backed, too quick-witted, too ambitious, too accomplished, too attractive to attractive women. He can still fly.

So maybe *About Schmidt*, then. Its gently rolling but not-dead-yet score could be mine, if anyone thought my life was worthy of a movie. The trouble with iconic actors like Jack Nicholson is that I usually can't see past the famous face. But Schmidt was real for me, from the establishing shot of him at his office desk waiting silently for the end of his last sedentary workday to him throwing out his back on a waterbed to him crying over the letter from young Ndugu in Tanzania. I don't know if you have children. I don't, but I've come to see my continuity in all boys and girls.

Food? Prime Rib. Spanish Omelet. Swiss Cheese. Chocolate Decadence.… I remember them fondly.

The six things I could never do without

…but have to. See above. Add hair. Also resilience and a few remaining principles. Without the one, I couldn't survive; without the other, I wouldn't want to.

I know, loan officers aren't thought of as principled. Funny thing: we used to be the villains for declining loan requests; now we're reviled for having accepted them. I know a lot of loans were handed out in the name of the American Dream, then foreclosed on when the subprime bubble burst. I'm ashamed for my profession, but that wasn't me: as far as I know, the people I put in homes still live in them; the ones I put in cars still drive them. That I never made management is a reverse badge of honor.

Remember those branch politics and the fired teller? Tellers are walking dinosaurs who already know that the asteroid is about to hit. Dating is not the only thing that has moved online. In the 2010s, mobile depositing climbed a thousand percent. And that's on top of ATMs taking over half of all deposits and counting. Tellers are now at a 40% share that's dropping like a stone. This particular teller was an old hand who'd seen the slide begin. He'd seen his hourly rate inch up over decades in which the cost of living soared. He saw neighboring credit unions pay their tellers one-and-a-half times that rate. He had reason to be vocal.

Management knew he did, but that didn't mean they liked it. They told him he had a bad attitude. What does that even mean, he asked. Don't bite the hand that feeds you, they said. Nobody feeds me, he yelled; I'm not a dog! And they fired him.

Until then I'd walked a line between the factions, but this disturbed me. I'd seen the man come in day after day for years, exchanged nods and small talk with him. Now his words, in the tone of a man at the limit of his endurance, rang in my head. I dropped in on the assistant branch manager, a generally level-headed person. But she shrugged and pointed mutely at the branch manager's office. A good decade younger than me, he said he respected my opinion but he'd been left no choice.

The teller may have felt the same. What happened next was unheard of, so no one saw it coming. Bank robberies still happen, though even that lovely tradition has gone online. Or, disturbingly, the victim of a predatory loan kills himself and/or his banker. But a teller? Our branch manager probably thought he was back to beg for his job. Instead he shot the branch manager with a handgun. Thrice. First in the chest, then twice up close, in the head. Then he shoved the barrel in his own mouth and splattered his brain across the office. The sound, indoors, was like fireworks. I won't disturb you with the other sounds. By the time a security officer rushed in, their blood had pooled together.

The next day I sat at my desk in a daze, then turned in my notice of early retirement. I could do without the job. It was killing us. The assistant branch manager, looking harried out of her mind, talked me into staying on for three months. And then, finally, I shed my suit.

I spend a lot of time thinking about
…the past, sorry. And yes, that includes the women in my life.

Funnily enough, not the women I was in relationships with (though I think of them, too) but the ones with whom I couldn't be. They hadn't lost all potential to work out, in my head, just most of it. That's "ones," plural. If it was just the one, you'd be worried. You'd move on to the next profile. Still here? I'm starting to like you. That potential to work out is still intact for us.

On a typical Friday night I am
Friday night, Monday night, it's all the same when you're retired. I was never a partier, anyway, especially once the bank stayed open on Saturdays.

That doesn't mean I don't get out. I don't want you to think I have no friends. When one stays single this long, a lot of one's friends wind up being empty-nesters or couples who never had kids. It's good to get male and female company in a package deal with no strings. It's bad, though, when a woman who's weary of being with the one man 24-7-365 makes it so apparent she prefers my company that it makes him edgy. Sometimes she's younger than him and still has the bloom. He enjoys that, but it makes him insecure and tired of the competition she attracts.

I, for one, know my boundaries, so they've seen that and settled down. Old dogs are less territorial. On the rare occasions I've brought a date, the men showered her with attention, and that was all right. Turnabout is fair play. So you might have that to look forward to.

The most private thing I'm willing to admit

Right. It's so private, I'll just put it online. Sure, it's anonymous, but not once we talk.

Here's a bad thing to admit on a dating site called OkCupid: I don't know about love anymore. It depends on so much. Timing, attraction, reciprocity, fidelity, durability, and so on. Two-way street all the way.

When the light on Stockton turned green, I wanted to stick around to see how it went between the blind man and the older woman. It looked like good timing and a great start, but who knew? Either of them might have had somebody waiting at home. As to attraction, it looked like they were feeling each other. Literally. But it might have been no more than the basic good-Samaritan interaction.

About attraction: its nature morphs as we age, doesn't it? In *Birdman*, Michael Keaton's screen daughter, Emma Stone, still in the first act of life, is horny for Ed Norton. At her age, all I cared about was how pretty and/or sexy a girl was. Norton, arguably on the verge of the second act, middle-age, is having relationship problems with Naomi Watts. By then, it wasn't only physical anymore. That part of it never went away, but sometimes I wished it would, that I wasn't so indiscriminately drawn to the bloom. Now I wanted a woman who was also kind, on the same wavelength, great company, and so on. Warning bells, not wedding bells, went off in my head at the slightest discord. Keaton, nearing the other end of that second act, is divorced, and even his fling with his stage costar, a younger woman, is failing. By that point, I'd come to terms with our inherent imperfection, my own first of all.

So here I am, at the start of the third act. And everyone knows, in general, how that ends. It's only the particulars that vary. My friends put it bluntly: "You're gonna die alone." I tell them I know. And I'm not the worst company. They've given up trying to set me up in the real world, bless them, but they sat me down to toss my hat into this virtual ring.

I'm looking for

See above. Microscopically detailed checklists are a problem, and they're ubiquitous online. Everyone's looking for everything, in some precisely imagined composite character. Height, weight, age, marital status, eye color, hair color, race, religion, location, education, occupation, income, nature, interests, sexual inclinations, sexual orientation, gender identification, sexual prowess—he or she must have it all. But s/he who insists on a 100% Match usually ends up in a sing-along with Bono: "I Still Haven't Found What I'm Looking For."

Take my first OkCupid date: we were a 95% Match. She was a well-kept brunette, bloom almost intact. Never married, no kids, sort of like me, but in her 50s, still in the workforce. Business writer for an insurance company. So we went to see *The Big Short* in the remodeled old Five Points theater, renamed SunRay because, hey, it's Florida. They've annexed a neighboring store and turned it into a second auditorium—have you been in it? Coziest little date theater, maybe five rows and fifty seats. We're sitting there in the semi-dark watching Steve Carell and company, sipping our wine, when I notice what she's doing with the large bowl of drizzled popcorn in her lap.

She keeps her face hovering over it, peering hard to sift and pick and toss aside or move to her mouth one popped kernel at a time, working rapidly but steadily, kernel after kernel, missing scene after scene. Occasionally she transfers a piece from the bowl to the running table in front of our seats, where it joins other discards. In the flashes of light from the screen, I can see them and they look fine to me. I've been in and out of the bowl for intermittent snatches, and all of it tastes good. My heart sinks.

Still, once she lays the bowl on the table, she's laughing at the financial machinations of Ryan Gosling and Christian Bale, so maybe the date isn't going badly. Except I'm not laughing. Just about then there's a vignette about Wall Street newbies trying to get in on the credit default swaps action. They're snidely put in their place by a hotshot insider. My date laughs again, so I crack a wry smile and say, "Schmuck." It takes a while before I realize that she has shifted away and stopped laughing, that she was laughing *with* the poser, not at him. I think. At any rate, I didn't survive the sifting. So much for the 95% Match. What the fuck, Cupid.

You should message me if
…you haven't run for the hills.

When the light turned green on Stockton, I dawdled with my eye on the sidewalk. No one behind me yet, though cars could turn off anytime from Riverside Avenue. The immediate question was this: now that the woman had stabilized the blind man, would the two carry on in opposite directions or would they proceed together?

Even as a small stream of cars took the turn, I got my answer. She swiveled around, linking her arm with the blind man's free arm. I cheered aloud and set my Sonata rolling. Across Oak, I swung into the lot of a convenience store reassuringly named Best Choice. Taking one of only a handful of parking spaces, chancing a tow if I wasn't back soon, I eased out and followed the pair on foot, a quarter of a block behind.

I reasoned there was a good chance the blind man had come from St. Catherine Labouré Manor, a sprawling assisted-living place back there by the river. In which case, she wasn't just taking him back to the home. And linking arms felt more intimate than if she'd taken hold of his arm. I saw that he'd folded his cane away, so now to someone who didn't know, they looked like any elderly couple out for a walk on a gorgeous Florida day.

Outside of the car, warm currents sifting through hedges and trees brought me their green scents. I tried shutting my eyes for a moment, and the fragrance grew, as did the sound of my shoes on pavement. The man and woman were chatting; I caught their companionable tone as we passed the Zencog bicycle store. Then they turned onto Myra, so I hurried past coffee drinkers outside Bold Bean, my original destination. My back and I were enjoying the unexpected exercise, and I was more interested in *their* destination.

Rounding the corner, I could see them again, closer now. I'd been down Myra before, even financed a home or two on it. It was a charming residential street with a random mix of houses. Wooden, brick, stucco, stone, burgundy, lime, blue, salmon, freshly painted, weather-stained, ranch, two-story, gables, terraces, porches, car porches, tidy, ramshackle, manicured, overgrown. But it worked. I could see either the man or woman at home here, and I was no longer sure which one it was.

Approaching Osceola, they slowed. Not to cross, but to turn onto a driveway. I quickened my pace. Behind palmettos and flowerbeds stood a modest single-story home in adobe with white trim. Its windows were trellised, its roof terra-cotta. I wished the man could see it. But the lawn smelled good, and, as I passed, I saw he was smiling. The woman was helping him over a pebble path, so that had to feel good. At the door, she let go of him to get her keys out. He stood quietly by.

True Fiction

AN OLD FRIEND FROM BOMBAY, unhappy with my loosely autobiographical stories, had this pointed instruction for me: "You should write true fiction."

I knew what he meant. He'd recognized an incident from our lives, though I thought I'd transformed it past recognition. Worse, he disliked a composite character whom he took to be his misrepresented self.

Still, struck by his paradoxical phrasing, I said, "That *is* what I write. Stories that are true. Not factually, emotionally."

"No," he said, and I could hear his aggravation. "You just muddle the facts. That's not fiction. You should make it *all* up."

"What good is it, then, if it's just made up?" He'd struck a nerve. "Do you know how many readers prefer nonfiction now because they know it's real? About real people, not vampires and zombies?"

"So write nonfiction. Write your bloody memoir, and make it real. Make us us."

Sure. I'd just be murdered by someone or the other who's in that memoir, for one reason or another. That's all.

"Right. There's no way I could get you right enough for you."

It's true. He'd asked me pointblank if that character was him, and when I said, "Of course not," his offended response was "Of *course* not?" It's a no-win situation.

"Secondly," I continued, "that muddling of the facts, as you so flatteringly put it, is what it takes to make a good story of our lives."

"Maybe *your* life," he said with a supercilious expression that, in all fairness, may have been in reaction to mine.

I dropped the argument—it was going nowhere. "All right, so *you* go ahead and write the memoir. Let's see if anyone wants to read that. I'll stick to stories."

But his paradox stayed on my mind.

Here's the thing about Arun. He argues to win. Not to get it right—he's sure he already is. Doesn't matter what the discussion's about; he's an expert even if he isn't. So if an argument doesn't go his way, he won't admit he's wrong. He'll just argue harder. And if cornered, he's not above muddling the facts himself.

I'm not sure when exactly that sense of omniscience grew within him. I can think back to before it did, when we were in short pants deliberating over deep-fried batwads in Campion School's noisy cafeteria.

"When you're thinking," I'd asked, biting through greasy batter into turmeric-yellow potato chunks, "you think in words?"

The question had occupied me ever since Mr. D'Sa told us in English class, "Choose your words, boys, not the other way around." The idea of words choosing me felt more exciting, and suddenly my mind filled with their sounds: *Choose... Chews... Choo Choo... Chook-Chook Gaadi... Giddy... Giddy-Up... Upma... Idli... Dosa... Masala... Messala... Ben-Hur... Chariot... Carrot...* Life revolved around food those days, even food I didn't like.

The look on Arun's face, a smaller, lighter-skinned, pretty-boy face long before it tanned and fissured, told me he was thinking about my question while observing that very thought for its nature. "Don't know, I just think."

"But like you talk? Like the words *batata vada* or how a vada looks?"

He looked uncertain. "More the picture?"

"In color or black-and-white?"

Already, he found the uncertainty taxing and replied emphatically: "Color! Taste, even."

He bit into his batwad, eyes narrowing to indicate the tasting process.

I suspect his self-confidence stemmed from being raised a mainstream, essentially ruling-class Hindu in Hindustan, not a congenitally insecure minority Parsi estranged in space and time from ancestral Persia. To his doting mother he was her "rajah," whereas mine fretted that Pervez, the name she'd given me, could be misconstrued by nationalist Hindus as Muslim.

Here's where I make the obligatory disclaimer that the names have been changed to protect the innocent. Except that there are no real innocents in a true story, unless there's a baby. Or a puppy, or a fledgling. And not even the last if we're talking cuckoo chicks. The cuckoo mom lays her large egg in a little warbler's nest or a robin's, rolling one of the unwitting host's eggs overboard. Clearly inheriting those ruthless genes, the cuckoo chick hatches, looks around at the tiny warbler chicks taking up space, and shoves them over the edge. It's a monster right out of the shell.

I'm not saying anyone in this story, young or old, is a monster. I am saying we're all complicated. Arun's early inquiries into the human psyche ran in a different direction than mine.

"You hate anybody in our class?" he once asked me. We were older, maybe in our senior year and now in long pants.

I trotted out the names of a couple of fellows I didn't like, but he stopped me.

"Really hate. Not 'don't like.' Hate."

So I tried to put some emotion behind one of the names. It felt good to vent about the kid who wasn't there to defend himself against petty accusations that I can't even recall. But Arun wanted more than rhetoric.

"Would you kill him if you saw the chance?"

The idea both shocked and intrigued me in its leap to the extreme. Nothing in between: not insulting nor punching nor kicking. Not even breaking his arm with a move we'd learned in self-defense class, a move forbidden by our black-belt Parsi instructor outside of an emergency. If and only if an attacker came at us with a raised knife or other weapon, we were to step inside, interweave an arm with his bent arm, and lever it back until it cracked at his shoulder socket. The attacker's screams were easy to conjure in our young heads, especially when our sparring partners brought us close to the edge. Now I experienced a perverse thrill from imagining my chosen foe *in extremis*, before the brutality of the vision jerked me out of it.

"*Kill* him?" I said, with a queasy smile. "Don't think I would go that far."

Arun nodded, looking faintly disappointed, but acknowledging reality.

SO IT WOULD BE WRONG TO SAY we grew up to be different—we always were. And so were our journeys. Our destinations, not so much. He married traditionally, a Hindu woman, yet ended up divorced, a trailblazer in those days. I married an American, having moved my Parsi ass to another country only to find that Iranian ancestry was more than a psychological issue here. And that divorce was as American as apple pie. I became an academic and a writer. He climbed the corporate ladder and, being Arun, climbed it to the top rungs of his multinational. Eventually, a step up from director of its Asia sector to director of the America sector brought him here, and he got in touch.

The third time he visited me in Florida, he called ahead to confirm, then unexpectedly called again. When I answered, he was already speaking to someone else, his voice businesslike and distant. He didn't hear me when I said his name a couple times, and I realized it was a pocket call. I was about to end it, but something about the muted conversation—its tenor, a note of tension in the voice of his subordinate—kept me listening uneasily. The recession had cut deeply into their profits, and the man was reporting on performance in the Northeast.

"What about this manager, what is his name, Pederson?" Arun asked. "How is he?"

"Yes, Pederson, Greg Pederson." The voice sounded Indian. "Good, no issues."

"Okay, but do we really need this position? Can the responsibilities be assigned to others?"

The man hesitated before replying in a guarded tone. "It's possible, but he is doing a good job."

"That's not the point. We have to do whatever we can to lower our expenditure, or we're in trouble. How much does he make?"

"One hundred and fifty. But he has a family—I know them—and he has given no cause...."

"That's one hundred and fifty thousand dollars a year that we can save. Let him go."

Silence from the man who'd have to do the dirty work. It was filled by the one who didn't know his old classmate was listening.

"Let him go." There was steel in Arun's voice.

"Okay." The tone was flat, careful.

I ended the call and put my phone away. A queasiness oppressed me the rest of the day. I'd been fired from part-time positions long ago, when I was the only one affected, and even that was no fun. I'm glad to have no employees to fire, no lives to potentially ruin. It bothers me when I have to fail the occasional freshman, even though he or she can take another shot at the course. Driving to receive Arun at Jacksonville International that night, I debated whether to tell him what I'd overheard. I wanted to ask how he'd felt, how he felt now. His tone had been impersonal and firm, but had it hid regret? Was he second-guessing his decision? An area director was probably under tremendous pressure to keep his ship afloat and on course. And a guilt-trip from an old friend could undermine his ability to make the tough decisions.

So I kept it to myself. He looked and sounded chipper at the airport, in a charcoal suit over light blue shirt. He'd either taken off his tie or hadn't worn one and had added some weight around the middle since the visit when he'd critiqued me. Cozy Tea was serving cozy dinner on the weekend, so I took him to Five Points for a British Indian meal of curry puffs and lentil pies, followed by bread pudding and chocolate truffles made in-house. I tried my rusty Gujarati on the family owners, and Arun added a word or two of vocabulary to his rudimentary "Kem chho?" before everyone fell back on English. It was dark outside when we entered my apartment. Once he'd settled into my guest room, he took off his coat. I mixed him a J.D. with Coke, and we surrendered to nostalgia. Old Campion pals and teachers, our ex-wives and marriage blues, his college-going son in Mumbai, the Brit-todesi name changes: Puné, Kolkata, Bengaluru, Chennai. Even some fun at the expense of my stories.

I think we were on our second drinks when he asked, "Did you find out if people think in words?"

My memory cells caught the reference, flashing back to our short-pantsed selves in the cafeteria. I smiled. There was something magical about a friendship that went back that far. "You remember that? I can still taste those greasy batata vadas. Man. But I can tell you *I* think in words. All the fucking time. My wife said I was too much in my own head. I think that would have bothered her even more if she'd known it was all language, just strings of manmade words and phrases and disjointed sentences."

It struck me that she and I had lived together for years without her ever knowing this. Or my knowing *her* mode of thought. Maybe it would have helped. "Still, I think I was just crossing over to that, back when I asked you. My favorite bit of communication ever was from a child, a lot younger than even we were, and it was wordless. Wordless, Arun. I wasn't actually in her head, of course, but it's not likely that the thought behind it came in words. I can tell you about it, and then you tell me what you think."

"Okay," he said, looking mildly intrigued. So I told him the story, in less detail than I'll tell it here.

It concerns an ex-girlfriend—several years before I met my wife-to-be—and her little girl. Before Mini-Me in *Austin Powers*, Morgan was Jodi's mini-me, to an eerie extent in someone so small. The pouty, entitled expression, the cool gray eyes, the honey-blonde, the retro cut, the whole effect enhanced by Morgan's larger-than-average head. Looking vertically down on the preternaturally self-possessed little creature, her two-year-old body and stubby legs further foreshortened beneath the bobblehead, you couldn't help but do a double-take from her to her curvy mother and down again.

When I first met Jodi, at a mixer after the First Coast Writers' Festival, she was by herself. She didn't say she was only separated—she said divorced. She was hot *and* interested, not a combination I got often, so I wasn't thinking beyond that. She didn't mention kids, and I didn't ask. There were some crosscurrents, though, over the wine and cheese. I introduced her to a writer friend who came sniffing, Ken Chambers, a deceptively laid-back dude until you played racquetball with him and he killed you. He was all over her, and she was flirty right back. In the meantime, I spotted a sweet old friend I'd always had a thing for, even after she married her boyfriend, unfortunately for me a good guy who made a good home for her and their boys. The impossibility of anything happening would normally have settled it for me, but the regret had turned out to be mutual and, consequently, lasting. Once we started to talk it was hard to stop wallowing in those frustratingly unspoken vibes. She had this wistful look, and I knew I did, too, until Jodi walked past us, saying pointedly to me, "I'll be outside." I nodded, said a regretful goodbye that was sadly returned, and stepped onto my rollercoaster with Jodi.

And Morgan. "Correct decision," Arun said at that juncture in my story. "Hot chick in hand trumps lovebird in the bush. But what about the little girl?"

"Have patience," I said. "A true story can't be rushed."

Still, he had a point. Jodi was if not first then foremost Morgan's mom. Before I even knew she had a daughter, let alone how important the mother-daughter relationship was to her, I could have read that in maybe the truest compliment she gave me. From the writers' festival, we gravitated to the Barnes and Noble by Regency. We wandered around the bookshelves, sat in the café for a bit, then emerged into the parking lot. The sun was still out and, after the air-conditioning, warm. The hopelessness I'd felt over my sweet mutual regret made me reckless enough to put a move on Jodi out there by her Subaru. She kissed me back, and I didn't want to come out of that exciting portent of new love back into the old ache. It was a long, *long* first kiss. When we came up for air, she smiled, a little cross-eyed, and said, "Mama mia!"

Every mother has been a daughter first.

I can't remember when she told me about Morgan. But I do remember the first time I visited the suburban home in which she and her ex spent alternate weeks, so that their little girl felt stable no matter which parent she was with. Jodi was receiving me amorously inside the door when a stubby little replica of her burst in upon us, saying excitedly, "Mommy, I went potty all myself!"

Jodi hugged her mini-me to her knees and congratulated her in the pleasantly surprised tone one employs with little children. Before we could be introduced, the child dragged her mother off to view her accomplishment. Repeated flushing sounds followed. But when Jodi returned to take me into the living room, she was alone again, permitting the resumption of our activities. I don't know if I was free-associating from the scatological interruption, but as we kissed, I cupped her rump with both hands. It was made for those hip-hugging sweatpants that used to say *Juicy* right across a woman's ass. As for her hips, Ken Chambers had said to me, "Man, Pervez, those are child-bearing hips."

My grab-assing audibly aroused Jodi as she pressed hard into me.

"Uhhh. So direct."

"Yeah?" I said.

"It's basically same-sex, you know."

"Same-sex?" I had gay friends even back then when homophobia was rife, but a guy's butt does nothing for me personally. I wouldn't pat one if I were a quarterback signaling the ball snap. Audio-visual cues for me.

Yet she nodded confidently before leaning in again. Long after we broke up, I saw her at an indie folk show being intimate with a gay woman I knew. So maybe she was preparing me for a bi world. As for us, we settled the matter pleasurably a couple of times the next week, first on my carpeting, then on my bed.

Post-coitus on the buff-colored carpet, she confided that custody details and who got the house were still TBD. The ex, whose name was Brent, had once picked up the phone when I called and sounded pleasant enough. He made good money in a downtown brokerage, not something Jodi, an adjunct at JU, could claim. So she was nervous about the upcoming court decision.

"What if I lose her?" she asked, turning to me as we lay there half-naked and sticky.

"Not going to happen," I said. "They won't separate her from her mother."

She snuggled closer. "I've seen it happen. And he's paying the bulk of the mortgage and rent. I don't know if I could afford even the apartment on my own."

In spite of her body heat, it took a moment before I could step up. "If it comes to that," I said, "you could move in with me. Little Morgan would love the guest room."

In all those single days I'd never lived with a girlfriend, except for the odd week at each other's place or on vacation. But Jodi's damsel-in-distress brought out my knight-to-the-rescue. And she rewarded me for it.

After that, it was often the three of us: at the zoo, the beach, animated flicks, carnival rides. All the fun stuff notwithstanding, I noticed that the exuberant little charmer I'd first seen had retreated into something of a sullen mute around me. She probably saw me as competition not only for her father, but for her mother's attention. So I received little to no direct communication from her. Jodi was our liaison, conveying the occasional whispered desire to me or repeating my inquiries to Morgan. In any case, Jodi's nightmare didn't materialize. She and Brent received joint custody of Morgan, and the house was awarded to her. I assumed that the settlement gave her the means to pay the mortgage.

"Good, good," Arun said at this point. He'd almost drained his second Jack Daniels, swirling the amber remains as I spoke. "Happy ending for mother and child. And in your roundabout way, you have come to the little girl's wordless communication. Still, Pervez, she was whispering to her mother, obviously in words."

I took our glasses to the counter for a refill. Ice cubes clinked in from the dispenser. "That wasn't it. But now I can get there."

I handed him his drink and settled back onto my couch.

Several months after Jodi broke up with me, I was at CiCi's Pizza for dinner. All-you-can-eat pizza buffet, dirt cheap? Made for a bachelor. Or, it turned out, a single mother. In walked a skirted Jodi holding little Morgan's hand. I winced; the breakup had been painful for me. Jodi had said some things. I'm hardly perfect, of course, and I'd admitted that to her early on in the relationship. I'm not a good communicator except in writing, so I'd tried to drop her a note now and then: emails, cards, even the occasional letter. The written me, I'd told her, was the most thought-through me and therefore, I felt, the core me, the real me, the best me. So she intended it to hurt when on breaking up she said, "You know what you told me about the real you being when you wrote things down?" I nodded. She shook her head. "It isn't. It's nothing like the real you."

I nodded again, my eyes dropping. She was probably right—the written me may just be the me I *like* best—but that didn't make it any easier to hear. And she hadn't only said things, she'd done some, too. I'll come to that later. Suffice it to say that something in me had hardened against her. So if I could have teleported out of CiCi's, I would have. But the entrance was also the exit. Morgan, in bright orange T over baby jeans, went to the candy dispenser while Jodi stood in a cashier's line. Then she helped Morgan around the buffet. Their plates filled with assorted slices, they came through to the tables, and Jodi spotted me. I raised a diffident hand. Right away, the old sullen look came over little Morgan. Jodi, on the other hand, looked genuinely pleased.

We caught up a little, and then, not to be rude, I indicated the vacant seats. "You're welcome to join me."

Jodi smiled and glanced down at her mini-me. "How about we sit with Pervez, Morgan? Would you like that?"

And for the first time since I'd known them, the tightly contained little girl threw a fit. A loud, arm-pulling fit, with angry cries of "Noooo!"

People turned to see what was going on. Clearly embarrassed, Jodi tried the stern route. "All right, Morgan, I've had enough of your nonsense. Stop it. *Now.*"

The child's shrill outbursts lowered to angry whimpers from beneath smoldering eyes. It hit me hard how averse she was to the slightest hint of her mother getting back together with me.

"It's okay," I said, as much to her as to Jodi. "We shouldn't force her."

A faint acknowledgment replaced some of the anger in those big gray eyes. As a compromise, Jodi suggested a table across the aisle. Leading with her stubborn little chin, Morgan nodded.

Everyone settled down to warm pizza for a while. My plate was an aromatic, mouth-watering mozaic of Supreme, Hawaiian, and BBQ slices, but I say that mostly from sense memory of past visits. My mind was not in the present.

I was brought back into it by a sudden materialization before me of the grave little girl. I must have appeared startled, because she looked up at Jodi by her side. They'd finished eating.

"Morgan says she wants to give you something," Jodi announced, and I sat up in surprise. "Go ahead, honey."

And with her miniature arm, Morgan held out a cupped hand to me. It opened like a flower to disclose two tiny objects. I leaned closer to look. They were translucent pieces of candy. Hard candy in the shape of yellow crescent moons. One was broken off at the middle, only half a crescent. It felt raw, touching. Indians give and receive sweetmeats as a token of goodwill, and here was this little American girl with an instinctive peace offering.

"Wow. Thank you, sweetie," I said, taking the gift and sliding onto my knees to gingerly hug the solemn little person. She didn't hug me back but didn't back away, either. "That's beautiful, thanks so much!"

Jodi smiled proudly down on us. And as they left, although I couldn't be sure, I thought Morgan looked just the slightest bit pleased.

"Yaar, let me tell you something." In the deepening night, Arun wasn't about to let this interpretation go unchallenged, though he did sound impressed with Morgan. "I know what you're saying about the mithai, but that isn't what the little girl meant."

I nodded and sent more J.D. down my gullet. "You're right, I didn't get it right away. I underestimated Morgan, just a two-year-old, after all. It wasn't happening to me in a story. No one had raised my expectations about her unspoken message. But as I looked at those two sweets, large and small side by side, in *my* hand now, the symbolism hit me. Stunning, from such a baby. Even then, Arun, at first after the fit she'd thrown I was paranoid enough to think she was telling me they were already a pair, just mother and child. No room for more. But then I thought of her gesture, so clearly an offering, and I realized she was saying here we are: we come together."

"Yes." Arun shook his head. "You were correct: it's fantastic."

We sat there for a second or two, argumentative old friends, nursing our drinks and the undeniable pleasure of being in agreement for a change.

Eventually I felt obliged to add, "It's also possible that…"

"Yes," he said. "Your girlfriend."

"Exactly, that she put her up to it. In that case, who knows in what form the idea came to Jodi. But just that the kid knew so instinctively what it meant, what she was saying without ever saying it.…"

"It's still fantastic." The guy wasn't arguing to win anymore. He wasn't arguing, period. "So after that did you make up with Jodi?"

I shook my head slowly. "More stuff had happened that I couldn't forget. Forgive, yes, but I couldn't put it all out of my mind and take the leap with her again. Remember Ken Chambers, the friend I'd introduced to her? We'd seen him again, several months into the relationship, and the way they looked at each other—you know what I'm saying?"

Arun nodded, and on his face there was sour recognition of where this was going.

"Male gaze is one thing when you're giving it," I continued, "and another when a friend's giving it to your girlfriend and she smiles and gives it back to him openly in front of you. Not bad-looking, Ken, athletic guy. A little after Jodi broke up with me, I got a call from him, all buddy-buddy. Turned out they'd run into each other at the library. He'd been surprised, he said, chuckling, by how really friendly she'd been. They were planning to get together again, and he'd called just to be sure I had no problem with that. Get it, Arun? He made it sound like it would be unreasonable for me to have a problem with it.

"When I said, 'Ken, you know she's doing this to make me jealous,' he said, 'No, no, I want you to know there's none of that going on.' He was probably right, just mutual horniness, but how could he know for sure? My point is he had every intention of going ahead with it no matter what I said. He just wanted my *approval*, too!"

Arun grunted. There was sudden intensity in his crow-footed eyes. "What did you do to the fucker?"

I shifted uncomfortably in my artificial-leather recliner and shrugged. The monthly cleaning crew had buffed its stone-gray with a free renewable cleanser from Rooms To Go. Its faintly alcoholic fumes mingled with those from my drink. Arun clearly expected me to have taken some punitive action. But Ken was at the other end of a telephone line—back then a landline. What was I supposed to do?

"Nothing. I told him, 'Do whatever you want to do—don't ask me,' and washed my hands of it. They deserved each other."

In Arun's judgment that was not enough. He sounded disappointed in me. But I had been quickly proved right. Ken called me *again* a couple of weeks later to recount his woes with Jodi.

"The woman was driving me crazy," he said, as if to say *you* know what I'm talking about. "She's obsessive-compulsive or something, just wouldn't stop calling."

I considered that unsolicited and unwelcome bit of information in the silence it deserved.

After waiting several seconds for me to respond, he had the gall to snap, "Is something wrong, man?"

"What do you mean?" The question packed all my pent-up anger and resentment, daring him to spell it out himself.

I could sense him back the fuck off. "Listen," he said in a changed tone. "You're upset right now, so I'll say bye. But give it time: you'll see. Sometimes things happen without anyone meaning anything personal."

And he was probably right. Jodi, who before long called me wanting to get back together, apparently had no clue why I wouldn't want to anymore. She just came right over and repeatedly asked me why. Finally I told her it was a combination of things, but it had really gone dead for me after the Ken thing. At first she nodded quietly, with a that-explains-it expression. But then she got mad at *me*.

"How dare you hold that against me?" she railed. "It was *after* we broke up."

Yes, but. So I said, "A) *You* broke up with me, and not in the nicest way. B) All I said was I didn't want to get together again. *You* insisted on knowing why. And C) I'm not 'holding it against' you. I'm just saying I don't have the same feelings after that. How does daring even enter into it?"

Startlingly she laughed, the bright, confident laugh of an attractive woman who knows her powers. She'd come over so fast, she couldn't have spent time on her appearance. But she didn't need to, with those gray eyes, those curves in a Jax Beach T and faded jeans. "You *know* you still have feelings for me. I'm going to keep after you until I wear you down."

"No!" I said, alarmed. I knew the power of a woman, too. "Don't do that. It's not going to happen."

This should have been her cue to leave. Instead, she slipped theatrically off my couch and onto the carpeting at the foot of my sofa chair, putting a hand on my knee. "What are you looking for, Pervez? Who's your favorite actress?"

I knew where this was going—not the first time it had come up with a girlfriend. A favorite actress, however unattainable, was an automatic threat. By definition more attractive, an irresistible ideal the boyfriend yearned for in spite of his girlfriend. Worse still if she was a different type. I reserved Holly Robinson for ethnic women. I'd gotten into trouble, once, citing Gwyneth Paltrow, as much for her acting chops as the rest of her. I could easily have done it again: Jodi was hardly a willowy lemon-blonde, and her face was more rounded. But something stopped me. It felt like kicking her when she was down, which she literally was. I couldn't even bring myself to shake her off my knee or just move away. So I compromised. I'd give her a hot actress to resent, but one with a rounded face, one she vaguely resembled.

"Angelina Jolie," I said, conscious of the mild disregard in which I held the curvy young star's thespian ability.

Sure enough, there was a slyly pleased element to Jodi's smile. "Nice lips."

I canted my head. "Yeah."

"I meant down there."

I did a double-take. "How would *you* know?" I didn't know about Jodi yet.

She kept coming at me. "Have you found someone else? Are you dating anyone?"

I could have lied again, but that's a lie I'd been told too often to use myself. "No," I said, resentful at having to admit it and wishing I *had* found someone. Like my sweet, long-time regret. Why couldn't *she* have gotten divorced instead? "But I might."

She nodded, looking pensive. "It's hard without someone."

"You have someone," I said. "You have little Morgan."

"Yes, thank God. But it's not the same thing. You're the only person I can really talk to."

"That's not true, Jodi." She was doing it, trying to wear me down.

She sat back, her heels underneath her. "It is—I'll prove it. I don't tell people this, for obvious reasons, but I'm telling you: I'm bipolar."

I opened my eyes. I should have seen it: on, off, mad, glad, bad, sad. But I'd only ever thought her moody, at most mercurial, even after Ken's amateur diagnosis. And *bipolar* was the latest buzzword, one that more and more people bandied about. Everyone had their ups and downs. I certainly did.

"Sorry, I didn't know. Are you on meds for it?"

She nodded.

"Man, Jodi, don't get hooked on those things. Just work through it yourself. Hold on a second." I rose and went over to my bookshelf. I picked out a self-help paperback on cognitive behavioral therapy, which had made sense to me but was too much daily work to keep up with. She was back on the couch by the time I handed her the book. It had an apple-green jacket. "Have you heard of this?"

She leafed through it as she spoke. "I've tried it. It didn't work."

"Keep it," I said, gesturing. "Give it another try."

"Okay." She sounded resigned. I guess she thought I was dismissing her. "Too much of a mess, huh?"

The honesty of that hit me. But I was still on guard. "No, I'm a bit of a mess myself—why else would I have a CBT workbook on my shelves?"

She stood up, her tone changing again: "Well, I gave you your chance, and you blew it. If you're not interested, I'm not interested anymore, either."

"That makes sense," I said sincerely. "Now stick to that."

And I saw her out to her Subaru. Neither of us went for a hug.

ARUN, MORE STRETCHED OUT NOW and still going on the Jack, didn't really care about this—he was fixating on Ken Chambers. "Pervez, you let that bugger off for nothing. He fucked you over, and you didn't make him pay for it."

"What the fuck did you want me to do to him?" Again my mind went racing back to Campion, to boys lined up against each other in white robes tied with sashes. "Break his arm?"

He smiled at that. "Good way to start off."

"Right, even that wasn't enough for you. So my turn to ask, big mouth. Did you ever hate anyone so much you killed him?"

Unexpectedly, disturbingly, I saw something shift in his eyes. Subtle but unmistakable. I'd triggered a recollection.

He took a swig from his glass and weighed his reply. When it came, those dark eyes looked straight at me, and there was a frightening emphasis on the opening pronoun. "*I* didn't kill him. But, ya, I hated somebody that much."

At a rational level, I was in disbelief. I was the expert on fiction: he had to be making this up, just to show me. *You think my life isn't worthy of a memoir?* Anytime now he'd break out a smirk: "Pulling your leg, man." Or maybe he meant he'd just *wanted* to do it, unlike actual murderers. Then I remembered his pocket call. Under certain circumstances, there was a ruthless Arun. Still, one thing to delegate a firing, entirely another to put a hit on someone. And if that was what he meant, did I want to know it? Wouldn't I have to do something about it? If so, what?

I drained my glass. My head swam and then one thing became clear: I didn't want to have to do something about it.

"So," I said, just as carefully, "what is it that you can't stand about Ken? I know he was a dick, but… Over the years I've actually come to feel that I acted as if I'd owned her."

Arun nodded. His shirttail was out by now, the lamplight casting shadows across his face. He looked into his drink and sighed. "Correct, he's not so bad. But suppose you and Jodi were married and you had the little girl together, and *then* he did what he did. Suppose you'd raised Morgan from a baby to a seven-year-old. A fantastic seven-year-old. Even now you're proud of her, and I see in some way you love her. Multiply by factor ten. Hundred. After all that, suppose the court gave her to her mother, and you could only see her on and off. Year after year after year without her, kept away from her for the next ten years of her life. Then what?"

I felt dizzy, sick. Moved *and* alarmed. Then what? And now what? I put my drink down. He'd told me his son was finishing B.Com. at Sydenham and had admission to NYU. I could see a lot of business trips to New York in Arun's future, and the need for his company to flourish in the States. Even at the cost of Pederson's job.

Now what? Now what? Every time I asked the question, my mind stalled. Between asking it, I took our glasses into the kitchen and emptied them. They clinked into the dishwasher. I didn't want to hear any more.

There are some true stories you just don't want to know.

He watched me as I walked back to the recliner. And I watched him. Again those crow-footed eyes never flinched. But this time I saw in them what I can only describe as a tortured expectation. He could not have spoken of this to anyone ever before. For more than a decade, he'd carried it inside him like an ulcer. Now, stunningly, he'd trusted me with it. Shared that terrible burden, transferred it partly onto me. But also taken the risk. A huge fucking risk, even with an old friend. And he was waiting to see what I would say, maybe what I would do.

For all the night's stillness, my voice was almost inaudible. "I didn't finish the story."

At that he dropped his eyes. When he raised them, the trace of torment was gone.

I find it telling, now, that not for a moment did I feel at risk. He just listened impassively.

There was no revenge on my part. Much good that had done Arun. Ken Chambers is fine sond doing well. If you're into dystopian novels and I'd used his real name, you might have recognized it. The writers' festival was defunded, so I'm thankful I don't have to see him annually. Our first couple of encounters post-Jodi weren't pleasant, even though the second was supposedly to "clear the air." His proposal, insincerely executed. But the third and last time, a few years had passed, allowing us to have a spontaneous and relatively friendly exchange. That's it. I don't care to spend any more space on him. This part's for Jodi.

She didn't take my advice right away. She didn't exactly stalk me, but she peppered me with emails. This was before social media. I kept my replies pointedly brief. She asked if I wanted to join a new yoga center at Bombaymeadows. Baymeadows, actually, but so many Indians live there and so many Indian restaurants sprang up that the joke name caught on. I declined but, remembering her bipolarity, encouraged her to go ahead and join. Next, she had a professional request. She'd started writing restaurant reviews for Jax papers and magazines and needed company to better sample a menu. I knew she could use the extra money, so I went along twice. And they were relaxed times, once with Morgan and once without. That second review, she wrote, "So there we were, a couple of sweet tomatoes at Sweet Tomatoes." Funny and, well, sweet. If not for my inability to trust her again, I'd have been tempted.

All of this happened in the half-year after our breakup. When it went nowhere, she finally dropped it, except that she emailed me every few months to ask my advice on departmental politics, her ailing Subaru, things like that. I always gave her the best advice I could, at length now—I felt I owed her that—but I never followed up. I couldn't tell if she was testing my resolve or reassuring herself that I still cared enough. At some point even those emails ceased. Years went by before I saw her with her friend at the Ani DiFranco show. I was with my wife, something of a feminist and a big fan. Ani played "Untouchable Face" that night, but there's no such thing. I thought Jodi looked a little tired. Happy but tired. Gaunt, even. I don't know if she saw me too.

More years passed. My wife and I split up. I'll only say it was probably my fault and get on with the story. I moved from our house in the burbs to this apartment in Riverside, a historic neighborhood become a grunge hangout become a new-agey hipster hood becoming gentrified. I live between a park on the river St. Johns and a duck pond that's more than a duck pond. Cranes, egrets, and geese flock to a little green island on the pond. They've come far and have farther to go, but here's a resting place. Watching them from a bench in the sun, taking in the river breeze, I'm more in the present.

On Sunday evenings I go to a yoga center, Avondale Ashram, to keep my sedentary paper-grading life from giving my spine a C. I've noticed that even in shavasana at the end of sessions, I can't stop that stream of language in my mind. It keeps me awake at night, so I get up and write or prep for class. One weekend the ashram held a meditation seminar. The owner is American, but he trained in India, and that's authentic enough for me. However Americanized his Sanskrit sounds, I appreciate his inclination and ability to code-switch. I went to the seminar, thinking the techniques might help. I wasn't alone. People from not only my regular session but all the other classes packed the practice room on its hardwood floor. Light chatter passed across our yoga mats.

Flanked by smoking incense, the owner got our attention to introduce a thin, middle-aged woman as the owner of Baymeadows Yoga.

"Hello," she said, looking around. "I won't hold up the seminar long. Some of you know Jodi Powell and have heard the sad news." I sat up, startled, not sure I'd heard the all-but-forgotten name right. "Her family in Wisconsin will be taking the body home, but we are planning a kirtan in her honor tomorrow at Baymeadows. You're all welcome, so please come."

And she went back to her mat.

My mind was scrambled. The Wisconsin detail confirmed it was Jodi. But what had happened? How could it have happened?

I turned feverishly to the shapely young woman in Lululemons on the mat next to mine. "Did you know Jodi?"

She looked curiously at me—I must have looked and sounded shaken—then nodded. "She was in the Sunday morning classes with me."

"Here?" My voice rose at the irony. I'd been coming in the evening. "At Avondale?" She nodded sadly. "What happened to her?"

She tossed a quick look at the instructor, but he was waiting for the slight buzz to subside. Still, whatever was on my face made her hesitate before, leaning closer, she whispered, "I'm sorry, it's the saddest thing: I heard it was by her own hand."

I couldn't find a single word. If I had thoughts, I can't tell you. I don't even recall an exact feeling, just a desperate jumble. I had no idea why I was reacting so badly, after all the time that had passed. I'm still not sure.

"Did you...?" The young woman was feeling her way along. "Were you and she...?"

I struggled to get it together. "A long time ago. I don't understand—why would she...?"

"All I know is they took custody of her daughter from her. Jodi stopped coming here after that."

Our instructor's soothing cadences began to guide the class into a meditative state. But my mind was raging. Why had they revoked her joint custody? How could they do such a fucked-up thing to an inseparable mother and child? Had her bipolarity gotten worse? Had she overdosed on the meds? Could those kill you? Did she mean to do it? And for god's sake *why*? Morgan would just about be a teenager by now. Another handful of years and that fucking custody battle would no longer have been an issue. Why kill yourself at, what, just forty-four, when you could wait out another five?

The pointlessness of it tore at me. Flash memories of things we'd done together, places we'd been to with Morgan, images I'd forgotten kept surfacing from long-dormant brain cells. I could see Jodi's smile, hear her voice and her laugh, feel her warm, vigorous, intelligent, seemingly unquenchable life as I hadn't in a whole decade. How could it all have been extinguished? How alone, how absolutely hopeless must she have felt? I didn't know when I started to cry. At some point I knew my face was wet, and I couldn't stop. I didn't try. I sat there cross-legged in an eerily silent room full of people and cried for Jodi.

I DIDN'T TELL ARUN THAT PART. But some of the emotion must have come through in the telling.

"It's tough," he said, less poker-faced now.

"It was." I wished I still had my drink. "A couple of things keep bothering me. One, even though she'd said it many years before this happened, that thing about me being the only person she could really talk to...."

His head barely moved in a nod. He knew what I was saying: I felt partly responsible for the solitary, silent, desperate place she was in at the end.

"It went bad, so you did what you did." He hadn't said that of himself. He'd more or less implored me to. "And you were still her friend. You helped her when she asked. Not your fault that wasn't enough for her. She found others. She had others. Where were they?"

"Thanks," I said. "I went to that kirtan for her at the Baymeadows studio. I was hoping to see young Morgan, a teenager and all, unbelievable! But neither she nor her father came. Maybe they'd gone to Wisconsin. May have been a good thing—I was angry at him, a man I'd never met, for taking her away from Jodi. I blamed him for what happened. I even wondered if Morgan's own testimony had helped the new court order along."

If it had, that's another story I don't want to know. I want to think it's impossible.

Arun shook his head. "The children are manipulated. Anyway, you see why I was angry." *My* anger, still evident, seemed to lighten his burden. He sighed for the second time. "Still it's better not—"

He broke off, startled by harsh, garbled cries that rang through the night outside. A woman was shrieking invective at the world, her words indecipherable beyond a barrage of F-bombs. I'd heard her before, when up late writing. Sometimes she was joined by a male voice, just as loud, engaging in an abusive call and answer, a kind of mating call gone wrong. Or a territorial one. Memorial Park by the river is legally closed at night but attracts its share of homeless people who've been pushed out of downtown. Some of them inhabit our streets in the daytime, asking for a buck or busking or rapping out apocalyptic sermons in the middle of the road. The regulars have become recognizable. A disabled veteran in the Publix parking lot takes your empty shopping cart off your hands. It's only when you ask that he salutes, then tells you of the VA's red tape. A stubby Asian woman lives on the sidewalk with a bulky shoulder-bag. But she's so quiet you can hardly hear her request. And so sensitive or proud that after I avoided eye contact once, she never asked me again.

Arun looked shaken.

"Homeless people," I said. "In the early morning you'll hear bird calls from the park. You know who else was there at the kirtan? Jodi's girlfriend, the one I knew before. Quiet, sweet, intelligent person, the kind I've heard described as mousy. And she looked as depressed as I felt. I was not the only one grieving for Jodi. But the chants went on and on, and some of it sounded so upbeat that I said maybe we should hear something in Jodi's own voice. Everyone nodded curiously, so I apologized for interrupting and read a passage from one of her pieces I'd found online. 'New Millennium Resolutions,' the need for a present-day understanding of ourselves. Then others spoke of how lovely she was, so friendly, so giving. Finally we all formed a circle and held hands for a minute of silence. The young woman from Avondale Ashram stood to my right, and I was too conscious of her hand to stay focused on Jodi. I came out of it feeling ashamed and disloyal. Unfaithful, almost."

Arun's gesture was dismissive. "The second thing that still bothers you?"

I thought back for a moment. "That confidence Jodi had? Her inner belief that she could set things right if she put her mind to it? My stubborn refusal to get back together may have started to break it down. Then when she was forcibly separated from the most important person in her life, I think she couldn't picture them reunited."

He nodded glumly. "Too much to bear."

The fierce cries outside had ceased, leaving a deeper silence. I looked at my downcast old friend, gravity creasing his face.

"I still have them," I said at last.

He looked up. "What?"

"The pieces of candy little Morgan gave me. I never threw them away, not even when I moved. Do you want to see them?"

When he nodded, I got up and went to my bedroom. I felt around in the dark for a second before locating the light switch. From my walk-in closet I pulled down an old suitcase. Rummaging, I found a ruby-colored little jewelry box that my wife had discarded. I opened and closed it to check for ants. Then I went back into the lamp-glow of the living room and set it down on my coffee table in front of Arun.

I snapped it open, and there they were on its plush blue bed. Two yolk-yellow pieces of hard candy, still together. The full crescent with beveled edges and the broken half crescent.

Steven

STEVEN MILLER IS WATCHING TV WITH HIS WIFE and kids when he realizes he is becoming a woman.

It's the finalé of one of the bachelor/bachelorette reality shows his wife Marla loves. A Kansas City Chiefs' cheerleader must select an "Average Joe" to be the love of her life. No pressure. After weeks of playing the field, it's down to a millionaire entrepreneur and a pretty-boy model, both of whom she likes the hell out of and only one of whom she must choose. Marla, who's an average Jane even to Steven who loves her, seems to identify with Melana, the gorgeous cheerleader, because their names sound alike. Names matter to Marla, who liked the alliterative sound of Marla Miller when he proposed fourteen years ago.

An ad comes on. Several seconds in, he has no idea what the product is and contemplates a trip to the refrigerator for one of Marla's wine coolers. His palate has gone sweet on him. Turns out the commercial's for soda: Sierra Mist, "refreshingly shocking lemon-lime." For reasons at first unclear to him, a Scottish marching band tramps along, bagpipes wailing. The men are kilted in plaid, and one is missing. Moans of rapture emanate from the set. The camera tracks to a Babe Ruth look-alike doing a Marilyn Monroe, his kilt flaring over the updraft from a grate. Steven gets it: Sierra Mist goes with Scotch in a "refreshingly shocking" way. More like comically gross. Yet something stirs, disturbingly, in his chest and groin. He feels at his shirtfront. It's rounded. He looks down to the crotch of his pants. It's flat!

His hands drop to his sides, and he sneaks a look at his family. Marla, Danny, and Jan have their eyes on the ad, snickering. On screen, a boy viewing the pageant gapes at the orgasming Scot and says to his father, "That's just wrong, Dad." The man shields his son's eyes.

Danny, whose voice is breaking, takes a bite from the pizza he prefers to regular dinner. Until a year ago, it was chicken nuggets. "Dad, did *you* ever wear a kilt?"

"Talking with your mouth full, Danny boy," Steven says absently. His voice sounds a tone higher, and he wonders if they noticed. It's not as if he had the deepest voice in the first place. "No, but then I was never in a parade. Nothing wrong with tradition. I think in Scotland it's still pretty normal. I'm told your grandmother's grandmother said she missed them—seeing kilts on men. She was just nineteen when she sailed from Glasgow on the *Caledonia*."

"Did she wear pants?" Jan asks, giggling. She's seven and very aware that she's cute. People say she takes after Marla, but privately Steven thinks she has his features.

"Long knit stockings, your grandma says, and they checked her hair for nits at Ellis Island. But women wear pants. Your mom wears pants; you know that. And you both wear jeans." He adds lightly, "Why shouldn't men wear skirts?"

Marla looks at him with a funny smile. The kids are cracking up: "Dad wants to wear a skirt, dad wants to wear a skirt."

"Didn't know I married a cross-dresser, Stevie," Marla says. She's on the couch with Jan, at an angle to his recliner, but he can tell from the way her hand opens and shifts along the backrest that she's mildly aroused by the thought. It has been a while since they role-played—before the kids came along, and even then they never thought of switching genders. Still, Marla's not averse to the girl-on-girl action in videos—she laughs at how it turns the guys on.

"Didn't know, either," he says, maintaining the light tone. It feels important to keep that going. "But you girls have all the fun: short shorts, skirts, tight jeans, bikinis."

"Omigod. You're not serious, are you?" she says, laughing uncertainly, then puts up a hand as the commercial break ends. "Quiet, everyone. I want to see who Melana chooses."

Melana is definitely conflicted. Adam, the millionaire, is funny and makes her laugh, while Jason, the model, turns her on when they kiss. Adam is undoubtedly an average Joe when it comes to looks, a good-natured, beer-puffed bloke, but he does kiss well, and she feels tenderly toward him. Jason was waiting tables before making the show, but he plans to return to school, and she approves. Adam is macho in a jokey kind of way. At first, Jason had to reassure her he wasn't gay, but after making out with him, she isn't worried. Both are clearly infatuated with her and have convinced her of that. It's enough to give Solomon fits, let alone Melana.

The kids settle down, and the show builds to when Melana must spell out her choice to each guy, in front of a jet waiting to take the winner to Cabo with her. Steven is a little in Adam's camp—he has been on the show from episode one, while Jason and the other good-looking anti-Joes came on later as a plot twist. But by the time Melana gets to Adam, who's all hope and anticipation, the rest of the world knows it's the kiss-off. She has searched within herself, and it's the way Jason makes her feel in the pit of her stomach that tipped the balance in his favor.

Marla doesn't quite know what to make of it. "She's right, don't you think? Gotta go with your gut. But he's not an average Joe! Shouldn't they have renamed the show? That's misleading, to call a show 'Average Joe' and then set her up with a chiseled, GQ type instead. I mean, Jason's nice and dreamy, but..."

"Yeah," Steven says. "Poor Adam. Though a millionaire isn't exactly an average Joe either."

He's not really into it—other things on his mind. The kids, too, are distracted: Danny by the private jet, while Jan is copying Melana's mannerisms. She thinks she's cheerleader material too, and football is big in Jacksonville.

Once they're in their bedrooms, Marla stops second-guessing the show and sheds her clothes for the night. Steven is nervous about shedding his; maybe it's time to confide.

"Marla," he ventures.

"Yeah, babe?" She's down to her bra and panties, and he can see the swell of her pudendum and the sideways bulge of her breasts. He's relieved to feel the familiar urge, even if it finds expression in his nipples and some crotch region not his penis. He can't tell if he still has one. He has heard of transgender women who chose to surgically remove theirs, and he's happy for them. To each his or her own. Dil in *The Crying Game* had famously kept hers, yet she'd broken Steven's heart. To him, the thought of not having his penis is alarming.

"You know how last week you said I needed a larger shirt size?"

She's in the bathroom now, brushing her teeth, and her words slosh around. "That's right, chubby. You must like my pasta." Then, clearly, his subliminal reminder kicks in. "Whoa, Stevie, were you serious about cross-dressing?"

There's the sound of hurried gargling, and her head pokes out of the doorway. The hair's a different shade of blond nowadays. Over the years, pores opened and her cheeks fell. The chin line now has a twin. But the eyes are still her, watery blue.

"Not really," he says, cautious, probing, "though what would you think if I was?"

"I wouldn't mind. Might be fun, so long as you don't go off the deep end with it. And not in front of the kids."

"Really? You'd be into it?"

"Well, once or twice, why not?" She giggles. There's the sound of running water, then it shuts off. "I kinda like the short shorts in classic basketball games. Guys wore these jogging shorts, right? And then only Richard Simmons wore them anymore."

"Mm." He considers this. What's happening to him seems different. It's not of his volition; it's just happening, and he wishes he knew why and what. He needs a look before he says too much. "Anyway, I've been wearing my roomier shirts and pants for a week now, so I think you were right."

"You have?" She's out, in her black nightie. It covers her love handles but not her increasingly fleshy thighs. He feels horny right away. "So what does the scale say?"

He crosses into the bathroom, swinging the door almost shut, then steps on the scale. "Um, up about seven pounds. One sixty eight, still okay for my height." He was a skinny one-forty at five foot nine, when they'd met in community college. Now they teach Comp and Lit at the University of North Florida. "But it's weird—at Dr. Barrett's last week for my allergies, they measured me at five-ten. That's an inch taller than usual."

"No way. Those nurses..."

"I don't know; their scale did read five-ten. Hey, remember that essay by Stephen Jay Gould in the *Norton Guide To Writing*? About a connection between animal size and gender?"

His fingers rush at the shirt buttons. All he'd registered, putting it on, was that he seemed flabbier every day. How was he to imagine anything else?

"Oh... You mean the one about the snail called something *fornicata*?" She giggles again, and it strikes him that she thinks this is verbal foreplay.

"Yeah, in Latin. The slipper limpet."

Then the shirt is off and he can't talk; words won't come out. Those are real breasts on his chest! He moves to the mirror. There they are: medium-sized, like Marla's original 33B, pert and pretty.

"Sounds right; I can't really remember. So what did it do, again? Something wild, I know."

He starts to unbutton the jeans and finds his voice again. It's strained. "They stack up on one another, like a pyramid of shells. That's not the weird part, though." The zipper's down, and he's pushing at the jeans. They're tight. "A young limpet—they're always male at the start—settles on a rock and gets the stack started. Then, as it grows, and smaller males settle on top of it, it turns into a female! When the ones above grow larger, they become females too. The smaller ones on top stay male, but their penises are so long they can reach around other males to the females underneath."

"Woo-hoo!" she hoots. "Now I remember."

He's looking down at the front of his BVDs. It's alarmingly flat—the front pocket would be flappy were the briefs not stretched at the hips. So much for once-upon-a-time long penises. He hasn't lost as much in percentage terms as the male slipper limpets, whose dicks, while they have them, are longer than their bodies. But that's scant consolation.

"You know, babe," she continues, chortling between words, "it's a good thing guys aren't like the limpets, considering how much I've been on top."

He's silent. Not only because he has been working her in the general direction and now that she's almost there he doesn't know what to say. But also, it's the moment of truth. Genitalia don't lie, and once he pulls down those BVDs, the bottom line will be there to see, either way.

"Sequential hermaphrodites," he finally says, procrastinating. "That's the term Gould used. And people can be hermaphrodites."

"Only from birth, I think." She sounds muffled, as if she has turned away. "I think the new term for hermaphrodite is intersex person."

He steels himself and shoves down the underwear. It's official—he's a sequential intersex person. Gone, the big Miller. His curly brown hairs now adorn the unmistakable inverted McDonald's M. He's the new owner of a pristine vagina.

NUMB, HE SITS TO PEE. It works as if he'd been doing it all his life. By the time he covers up with his loosest pajamas and emerges, Marla has slipped under the bedcovers. A wicked smile tells him she's horny. He goes around to his side and gets on top of the sheets. The table-lamp is best left on; switching it off would automatically signal snuggle-time.

"Did you actually shave for me, Stevo?" She reaches out to stroke his smooth cheek.

"Sort of." He'd shaved that morning, and there had barely been any stubble.

She smiles again. "You're so strange today. I like it."

He can't hope for a better segue. "Um, Marla... Fact is, I *am* kinda different."

"I know it!" she says. "It's all right, baby; I told you I don't mind. Trade your jammies for my nightie?"

He considers. Would that soften the shock or worsen it?

"It's not exactly that. There's something else going on, I don't know what."

"Stevie, what is it?" she asks, sobering visibly and sitting up. He must have lost the lighter tone. "Are you sick?"

"I'm not sure."

"Oh, honey, you should've told me. I forget to wash, too, after grading papers with those kids' germs all over them." She moves to hug him. He leans back from the hug, and she looks hurt. "It's okay, I'm not going to get it from you; I've been taking my Echinacea and drinking OJ. Do you have a temperature?"

She puts the back of her hand to his forehead—the hand feels cold to him.

"You're feverish, babe," she says and hugs him close before he can stop her. She pulls up and stares at his chest like she can't believe what she just felt. Then she looks up at him, and he looks back. Her hands come around to his pajama shirtfront. And she shrieks, springing backward.

"Shh," he says, "the kids... I was trying to tell you."

"What in God's name was that, Steve?" she says through her teeth. She's shaking. "Is this one of your practical jokes?"

"I wish," he says morosely.

A picture is worth *et cetera*, so he pops the pajama shirt buttons and peels the flannel over a pair of pink nipples. Damn, he thinks, they look good.

"Oh God, oh God," Marla says, her hands at her mouth. "When did you do this? How could you do this to me?"

He buttons up hurriedly. "I didn't do anything. I'm trying to tell you, it just happened, I don't know how."

Her eyes waver, like she's trying to believe him. "Okay... 'Cause if... if you did, you can always change it back. At least I think you can. Oh God, I hope you can." She's back on that track again—it's easier to deal with. "And then, whatever needs you have, you've just got to *talk* about it before you go off on your own and... and..."

"Listen, Marla." He can feel the heat take hold of his head and rack it. "You've got to trust me on this—I had nothing to do with it! Who do you think you married?"

"That's what *I* want to know," she says, a bit sullen. Then the slightest gleam of curiosity creeps into her eyes. "Is it all the way? I mean..."

She peers uncertainly at the crotch of his pajamas, which is almost covered by the shirt.

"Yes, it is." He doesn't have it in him to elaborate.

"Oh no, Stevie," she cries, "I loved the big Miller so much!"

He grunts, not meeting her eyes. "More like lil' Milly now."

She puts a hand out to his arm, but keeps her distance otherwise. "I don't know what to say, it's so weird. Why do you think it happened?"

"I'm trying to figure that out. Remember I told you about my Uncle Rick who vanished when I was a kid, just sold his house and went away without a word to anyone? How he'd gotten so flabby up top, Mom and the others teased him about having boobs?"

"Yeah, wow," she says. She seems to be settling into some form of calm. "You think he was a... a sequential...?"

"I don't know, maybe," he says, suddenly tired. "It's the best I can come up with. I'll go see Barrett at the clinic tomorrow, though damned if I want to tell anyone else about this. Listen, I'm going to take some Tylenol and be back."

"All right," she says uncertainly. "Could you also check on the kids? I need to think a little. A lot."

He looks at her. Their policy on tackling the bigger problems is to do their thinking together, as a couple.

"You know I want to be there for you," she adds quickly, "but my mind is going like crazy. This isn't like you just had an urge to wear a skirt, you know?"

"I know," he says. "I'll check on them."

THE TYLENOL'S TAKING ITS TIME KICKING IN when he opens Danny's door. The light is off, and Steven feels his way though the dark until his eyes adjust. It's a journey he's made before; he keeps his left arm out so his fingers guide him past the edge of the dresser. The bed's outlines appear. The slight figure beneath the sheet looks relaxed, its breathing regular. The head becomes visible, its delicate lines, the longish hair. Steven remembers when guys at community college and UF gave him a hard time for his '70s hair. But Marla liked it; she complained when he cut it once they started to teach. The thought gives him hope.

The light is off in Jan's room, but she calls out as he enters. He replies and gropes his way to her side. Her warm, small hand takes hold of his in the dark, and it's as if the Tylenol kicks in. Quick on its heels, pinpricks start at his eyes. He holds them back. Surely Jan will still love him.

"Dad," she says. "Do you think I can get on the Roar when I grow old?"

"You bet, sweetie," he says. The Roar is the Jaguars' cheerleading squad. "When you grow up, not old. But heck, why only cheer when you can play?"

They talk about it for a while. Then he squeezes her hand and leaves.

Marla has shut the light. Good idea. He makes his way to the bed. She's awake, he senses, too quiet. He positions himself neutrally, looking up, neither turned away nor toward her. Then he waits.

"Steve," she says.

"Yeah?"

"Swear you had nothing to do with this?"

"I swear it, Marla. You're bummed, I know, but how do you think I feel?"

"I don't know—tell me."

He's silent. Fuck it. Thirteen anniversaries, and they might as well be strangers.

There's an upheaval on her side, and he can faintly see her tipping onto her elbow. "I didn't mean it like that," she says in her voice of capitulation. "I know it must be crazy for you, too. It's just I'm so confused."

She has put out her hand in the dark, a risky venture now. But it lands safely on his stomach, and the way it just sits there comforts him.

"Welcome to the club," he says.

"I was thinking: while we're figuring this out, why not..." She hesitates, then starts again. "I used to wonder what it's like for two women. I mean, we've seen videos and all, but..."

"Yeah," he says. She's horny again. It feels like acceptance. He has a flare of arousal himself: this is going to be different.

Her hand moves again, under the flannel and over his stomach. Her lips come down on his, plump and hot. The hand is still moving—whoa!— squeezing his breasts. Lightly at first, then hard. Automatically he reaches for hers, but his mind is on the new sensations. She has his nipple now, and it's standing up against the flannel.

She stops. "Stevie, I should have asked, is this okay with you? Am I being insensitive, coming on at a time like this?"

"Hell no," he gasps, "don't remind me. Come on all you want."

"Okay," she says, and one hand begins to work down his pants. "I'm so turned on, it's weird."

He can hear her breathe as she encounters the newest pussy in the house. Then all other senses are lost in the touch of her fingers, as she does to him what he's seen her do to herself and has learned to do to her. She slides down his belly, and her lips and tongue join the fingers at work. His thighs spread, juices squirt, and it's only his recollection of the Sierra Mist commercial that keeps him from emitting noises.

All of a sudden, she's scrambling off him, and he hears her rummaging in the dresser drawers. Then she's between his thighs again, using his emissions to wet what he knows is her favorite dildo. It's pink. And long. She spreads him, probes with its head, and inserts it. Holy mother of... It pushes his walls apart inch by inch, and as she begins to thrust, two thoughts go through his mind. Was that a hymen? And: this is what it's like to be fucked.

THREE WEEKS LATER, THE SEX IS STILL GOOD—he doesn't want to think of it as great. Marla has purchased a strap-on, who knows where, and is developing quite the repertoire of moves with it. She gives it to him to try, but it's not the same. The dynamics feel old, forced, a pale imitation.

Other things are not so good. Once Dr. Barrett gets past an understandable belief that Steven has had surgery, the G.P. is intrigued but baffled. He makes noises about reading up on it, and schedules Steven for diagnostics at the Baptist Medical Center, all of which turn up normal. For a woman. Then he refers him to an endocrinologist on the south side, Dr. Sanchez, who is equally baffled but eager to start him on hormone therapy and chronicle the case.

She's not the only one—Marla is taking notes. She feels that with life material like this, maybe she can revive her aspiration to be a stand-up comedian. Stand-up routines are often about spouses' quirks, and Steven has gone way past quirky. One evening after an episode of *Last Comic Standing*, he sees this one-liner on her notepad: "My husband and I practice the rhythm method—he fucks me after I ovulate, and I fuck him after *he* ovulates." He's relieved on one count; it's not the greatest joke. It's not even true: the scans at Baptist show that he has ovaries and a womb, but for some reason he hasn't yet menstruated…maybe they've started the hormones just in time. And she's missing the point; they don't need contraception anymore. On the other hand, the quip is troubling in that it seems to confirm what he thinks during sex—that she's fucking him for having changed on her.

Danny doesn't know. He's past the age for hugs, and his mind's on other things—like girls. He and his buddies have started hanging around girls in class and the Kensington neighborhood. Some of them wear baggy pants so loose that they slide down their shorts, puddle around their shins. The girls come by as much as the guys, now, to ask for Danny. If they notice that his dad seems to have filled out like them and adopted a roomier line of wear, they don't mention it. Little Jan's into hugs from daddy, of course, and at first Steven sees a quizzical look cross her face. But for all she knows, fathers are probably supposed to change like that, so she hugs and kisses him all the more. He was right about her; she's still his sweetheart.

What exactly he is, he's not so sure. A kind of human slipper limpet. He assigns Gould's essay to his Comp 1 class at UNF. In the men's rooms, he goes straight for the cubicles. When students or colleagues say he sounds different, he tells them he's stuffed up from allergies. It's true. No one asks about his new look. Prepping for class, he reads that the basic, original gender is the egg-carrying female. The male evolved later, to spread the genes more efficiently via hordes of tiny, low-maintenance sperm. He pauses over a piece of trivia: the egg of the leopard gecko develops into either the female or the male, depending on whether it's incubated at 77 degrees or 98. In humans, it's the balance of hormones that does it—more estrogen results in two X chromosomes. His heart lurches. Dr. Sanchez has started him on testosterone shots, but surely his chromosomes were established thirty-eight years ago in his mother's womb?

Speaking of, he needs to call his mom in Memphis and ask if she ever heard from Uncle Rick after his final visit when Steven was six. But he's not ready to tell her she now has a daughter. As it is, she gets an annual call from his father, whom she has never forgiven for leaving but who calls anyway, driven by guilt. Steven came to terms with their split when in his teens, and could probably let his father in on his new status. But his mother—who, maybe symbolically, has reverted to her maiden name, Dunn—would be even more upset if he didn't tell her first.

"Pop quiz," he announces in class, to groans. "On 'Sex and Size.'"

He sits at the desk, after distributing the quiz, and looks around at the bowed young heads. These were his kids even before he had Danny and Jan. Each new semester he'd felt like big brother at first, then surrogate dad of a hundred teenagers. He looked eagerly for faces that had followed him up from freshman Comp into Intro to Lit. The first time twins were on the roster, they became *his* twins. That Rashaan and Akili happened to be identical was just the frosting—when they razzed him because he messed up and called the one by the other's name, there was something easy and intimate about it. They were a favorite topic with Marla at home; he made a big deal of it when, in their very first year, they made the UNF Ospreys. He went to the Arena to watch and, after the games, to josh them about missed baskets. When neither of them was drafted by the NBA, he took it personally.

Heads are lifted now, eyes on him, hands idle. He looks at his watch and sounds the one-minute warning. An invisible stream from the air duct plays around his nose, triggering his allergies, until he shifts his chair. As the minute expires, some students are still scratching away, so he waits until the second hand goes around again and their pens are laid down. Then he collects the quiz and backs up against the desk to review it.

"That is such a weird essay," Linda Quinn says from a back row, inspiring a general murmur.

"I'll give you that," he says. "But in what way, exactly?"

She looks around and giggles; her braces catch the panel light. "All of those things changing sex."

He joins the sympathy chuckle. "So not so long ago we thought the genders are cast in concrete. What does paleontologist Gould say—does nature intend that?"

"Not always." It's Jason Zamito, to the left, one of the surfer dudes, a sun-streaked blond in flip-flops. "There's all these snails 'n fish 'n plants that cross over as they get bigger."

"That's right, in two ways. Protandry—male first. And protogyny—

female first." Sounds of relief and dismay over the relevant question. He moves on to the next. "What's Gould's thesis? Which way's more common and why?" Several hands go up, one of them attached to a flirty brunette who always takes a seat right in front of him. "Valerie?"

"Um, I wasn't sure, but male first? 'Cause females are usually larger— 'cause eggs need to be larger than sperm and need more protection?"

"Good job," he says, and she rewards him with a smile. "Yes: excepting mammals, nature favors the larger female. Anyone wonder why even we, when we hit puberty, the girls are taller?"

There's a chorus of Ohhhs, and Jason says to Valerie, "But then the guys get bigger because we had to hunt 'n fight and get you to date us."

"Ha ha," she says. "Dr. Miller, don't you think women were always smarter than men? That's how we got them to do things for us."

"No way," Jason says. "You couldn't survive without us, so we took pity on you. Right, Steven?" He's too cool to say Dr. Miller.

Steven waits for the ripple of snickers to die, then says, "Well, guys, I'll tell you what." He loves how usage has transformed the word *guys* into universal address. "Three hundred million years ago, before there were chromosomes, there were autosomes—think A for asexual or androgynous. Go back far enough and there was no battle of the sexes...because there were no sexes." He has their attention. "And the world goes around. The male chromosome, the Y? Sorry to be the bearer of bad news, Jason, but it's in a state of decay. It's the one that may not survive. Look ahead far enough— oh, about ten million years—and the Y may be gone."

Pandemonium.

"Relax." He's grinning now. "That's many more millions than we've been around as a species."

They quiet down, and Andre Martin speaks into the silence. "You saying there won't be men anymore, just women?"

Andre has invited Steven to the River City Gay Pride parade. Maybe he can tell.

"Not necessarily," Steven says. "There are male rodents who come by their masculinity without the Y chromosome...no one knows how. So I wouldn't worry too much about it." Ironically phrased—he's extremely worried. "Now let's talk about thesis as a principle of selection and arrangement."

AFTER CLASS, VALERIE HANGS AROUND, exuding femininity, to ask questions they both know are less than urgent. In the past, he has twirled his wedding band to send a signal, but she stays persistent, even now. It's a mystery. He's reflexively attracted to her, her tight young curves, her unlined face, the way she looks up to him, the flattering attention to his every word. He has seen other Valeries come and go, learned to squelch the physical attraction by noting the different planet on which they live. But now he has a new, unexpectedly vexing recognition: it's not just the thought of Marla or his ethics, anymore, that would keep him from taking advantage of Valerie—it's also the fact that he can't. Not in the way she'd expect.

She tags along as he navigates the café quadrangle, weaving between outdoor tables and lissome, sun-bared legs. Everywhere, young people sit by each other, buzzing with sex. He remembers when Marla and he first sat on the stone benches at Kent Campus, heads together, generating visions so tangible that for years they came true. Between the old love song, "Danny Boy," and Marla's affinity for rhyme, the kids' names—and genders—were decided long before they were physically conceived.

He gives Valerie the slip at the UNF bookstore. Then he walks up to the department and drops in on Marla. She's at her office desk, prepping for her afternoon Lit class, and looks more surprised than glad. Lately they only see each other at home. She has on a new blue top over a black skirt and has lost a little weight. She looks younger, more stylish, less the average Jane.

"Hey," she says.

"Hey. Thought I'd drop by for a minute."

"Yeah?" She looks almost like he'd caught her at something. His eyes search for her comedy notebook, but it's the bulky *Bedford Introduction to Literature* on the desk.

"You're not using the Norton for Comp, are you?"

"No, I'm trying the *Short Takes*. Why?"

She's clearly not going to invite him onto the second chair, so he pulls the door shut but stays on his feet. "Remember, aside from the slipper limpet, Gould talks about this plant, the jack-in-the-pulpit?"

"Sort of. I never quite got how the gender thing applied to plants."

"Well, yeah, most are simultaneously male and female, androgynous if you will—stamens *and* pistils in their flowers. Funny how 'pistil' sounds like it's the penis, when it's the other way around." Her eyes shift, and for an instant he's distracted. "Anyway, some plants' flowers, like the jack-in-the-pulpit's, have just the one or the other. In other words, they're either male or female at any given time."

"You know, Steven,"—she sounds suddenly tired—"I'm really not in the mood for botany, biology, whatever. And I've got to finish reading up before lunch."

"I know." He makes a token move toward the door. "Just one thing, then I'll go: when the jack—when Jack grows past a certain height, he turns into Jill. Old news, right? But guess what? When Jill is trimmed or grazed on or deprived of sunlight and becomes shorter as a result, she turns into Jack again!"

"Oh." Marla's eyebrows, still the original blond, are up.

"So this sequential thing, it's reversible."

"Babe..." Her voice and face have gentled. "I hate to break this to you, but how do you propose to be grazed on or trimmed? Or are you planning to get less sun?"

"I don't know how, Marla," he says, his throat tightening. "But that's par for the course. We don't know how I grew taller in the first place. Like remember how I had a fever at the time? If I catch the chills instead, lower my body temperature..." He catches the look on her face. "Okay, I know. That's just an example. My point is who knows? All these testosterone shots at the clinic. So far so good: no period, no nothing. Can you see my facial hair? I almost need to shave."

He pauses for confirmation, but the best she can manage is an uncertain nod.

"So there you are," he says. He needs to sound confident, not desperate. "Speaking of the shots, I'm due soon. Want to come along?"

She hesitates. "Maybe another time, when I don't have class. But let me know your height when they measure you."

Her eyes meet his directly, with only a hint of cloud. He drops his, understanding.

For a moment, he sees nothing but desk; the wood grain has these crazy patterns. One day, when he was six, his Uncle Rick came over for dinner at their Memphis ranch house. They never saw him again. Steven's mother rarely speaks of a later day when her husband left, but she swears her brother, new breasts and all, had a kind of dignity that final night. He ate steadily, with his head down, putting away her stew and turnovers. Twice he mentioned their Grandma Kathryn, how she'd set out on that long voyage from Glasgow so young. At the door, he shook his brother-in-law's hand and hugged his sister. Then he lifted Steven above their heads and held him there, close to the ceiling, before setting him down.

Marla is already turning away, back to her text.

"I'll do that," he says. His voice comes out quiet, almost resigned.

And he leaves to be measured.

The Straight

WNF SAW THE ROUND ROLLING ALONG the straight a while before they met. Time enough to weigh his options. The flat looked around, keeping it casual. Sunny and warm though the revolution was, he knew it could be his last.

They were the only ones on the straight. And the round looked too big to cover. Wnf flapped along a little slower. He felt the round, too, had slowed her roll. To one side of the straight were a few open highs, to the other a public broad. So she had enough opportunities to avoid him.

She took none, and the flat readied himself.

"Wnf," he said, when they came abreast. She smelled like fluid.

"Mlp," the round responded, wobbling affably.

"Hello, Mlp," he said, encouraged enough to be up front with her: "Well, what do you think?"

"I've seen worse flats," she said with a wobble. "But my found used to say one should always take the tour…. Show me what you've got, Wnf."

The reference touched him. Past tense applied to his found as well, though he couldn't recall a pithy saying of hers to bring her alive. He considered invoking Found's Zkian accent and choppy speech, but discarded the thought in favor of taking the invitation.

He flapped a corner. "Your found was wise."

And with that, he stretched every corner to the limit, and then he stretched some more. When he was done, he was big enough to cover Mlp. Exhilarated, he popped out his sharps and flapped them at her.

"So cool," she said, wobbling like crazy.

But the display had drawn others. Another round, not as big as Mlp, rolled off the broad toward them. And a second flat, possibly bigger than Wnf before stretching, flapped out of the carved opening to a high.

"Rsj," the flirty new round said.

"Wnf," he said, talking over the other flat.

It didn't work. "Mlp. I'm sorry, I couldn't hear you."

"Gxh," the rival flat repeated. "Nice to meet you, Mlp. And Rsj."

Wnf's sly flap barely moved the gas. "But not me, huh?"

Gxh just launched into an aggressive display. His sharps popped before he even stretched his corners. At full, he was bigger than Wnf. And he kept right on flapping. Then Wnf flapped too, harder and harder, directing it at both rounds. With every flap, the frequency rose until they were vibrating, putting out hums that wove over and under and around each other.

The rounds were rapt.

But Rsj, the smaller one, wanted more than just show. "Take it to the next level, guys. C'mon!"

Ready to go, chemical coursing through their tracts, the flats turned toward each other like buzz-saws.

"Wait," Mlp screamed. "Retract first—retract your sharps!"

Rsj rolled. "Oh please. Let's have it all the way."

Mlp turned on her furiously. "Easy for you to say, you stupid twit."

"All right, then." Rsj rolled some more. "Let's hear it from *their* cords: are you guys up for really settling this or not? 'Cause that's what I want—a real flat!"

The flats had paused, their hums trailing off. But at that, Gxh fired up again, keening high over Wnf's wavering drone.

"How about you, Wnf? You strong enough to be my flat?"

"Or dead enough for nothing." Mlp's tone switched from scorn to pleading. "Be smart about this, you guys, please!"

It got to Wnf. He retracted his sharps, stilled his flaps. The drone died, and he was at Gxh's mercy.

"No backing out," Gxh roared. "Use the sharps or I will!"

Fighting his survival instincts like crazy, Wnf simply lowered his corners. "Do what you want. I'm done."

A period passed.

Then Gxh trumpeted his triumph. The sound echoed off the highs and across the broad. Strollers turned to check. Dwellers peeked outside, seemed to recognize Gxh, and withdrew.

Rsj rolled over to him, wobbling seductively. "Let's go, Gxh."

"Yeah," he said. "Forget these losers."

And they disappeared into the carved opening.

Conflicted, his chemical still high, Wnf turned to Mlp. Taking her in again in the palpable silence, he felt better. Something about her was beautiful. To him, anyway, and that was all that mattered.

"That was exhausting," she said.

He lifted a corner. "I'm glad, now, that you stopped me."

"It was brave of you to stop. I was scared for you."

They paused, still seeing each other afresh. He could smell her fluid once more.

"My found grew up in Zk," he said eventually. "She didn't say anything as memorable as yours did, but she had an endearing accent to her last revolution."

Mlp wobbled at him. "I wish I could have heard it! Love to hear more about her."

"Love to tell you."

"Listen, I'm famished. Let's go find a place where we can ingest some solid while you tell me about her."

"Makes sense," he said. "Can't have you feeling exhausted *and* famished. Which way should we go?"

"I passed a small place a ways back. Nothing fancy, but it'll do. Unless you have a better idea?"

"Nah, let's do it."

He put a corner to her as she swiveled close, so close he felt chemical shoot through him as they set out together along the straight. It stretched past the highs to a hazy horizontal. Wnf felt he could see the distance the straight would take them.

What was undoubtedly happening right now between Gxh and Rsj would also, sooner or later, happen with them. For all of Gxh's machismo, he was not destined to stay a flat. Nor was Wnf. He and Mlp would get it on. In a high somewhere, he'd stretch to his utmost, flap like a demon, pop forth his sharps, and cover her. She'd absorb his sharps into the density of her fluid, deep, deeper, until they were humming warm surface to warm surface. The hum would become a keen as the sharps locked. Forever. At fever pitch, pods would fill with fluid and push out of his back, now their unified front.

Then, neither flat nor quite round anymore but at last a found, they—she—would roll out of the high and along the straight, ingesting way more solid to build her strength and feed the pods. Orbits would pass. The pods would expand and, eventually, split open. Little flats and rounds, inhaling their first gas, loudly exercising their new cords, would drop to the straight to be nudged and nursed by their found. Ingesting fluid like little gluttons, they'd grow. Soon they'd get on solid and grow some more. Flapping and wobbling around, they'd look up and say, "Fa?"

Almost bursting with pride, their found would yell, "Yes! I'm your found. Found. Can you say the D? Founduh. That's right: found."

More orbits would pass. She'd raise them to be good kids, keep them from wandering off the straight. She'd keep them safe. All the dangers pressing in from the highs, blowing hard off the broad, she'd keep those at bay. Inevitably something would get past her, and she would not be able to save them all. She'd have to get over that fast, put up her guard again, and keep them moving along the straight. Keep them fed. Keep them happy.

Keep them learning. Until one fine revolution they'd be grown, the rounds as big as her, the flats bigger, protecting *her* now, all of them, fending off danger before she even knew of it.

Yet danger would sneak up on her from the one place they couldn't guard: her insides. Right about then, with her replacements—Wnf's and Mlp's replacements—firmly in place, the universe would deem her superfluous. Built-in expiry dates would pass, self-destruct mechanisms would kick in, and she'd start to implode. Slowly. Painfully. Unstoppably. Her very fluid would evaporate, leaving her a weak, shrunken raisin, until one sad revolution they'd all gather around her, and she'd say her last goodbyes.

After she was gone, the brood would lose cohesion, spread out a little, maybe cross the broad, travel other straights. A few might even reach Zk. Her handsome flats would meet rounds along the way, her beautiful rounds would meet flats. They'd say, "You know, my found had the faintest trace of an accent. Not all the time, just some random word now and then that sounded a little different coming from Found. I could never quite place it. Until now! I honestly think, listening to you, it may have been Zkian." Charmed, their new friends would flap or wobble encouragingly, then ask for the tour or give it.

And life would continue.

Family Tree

I
Family Story

Family tree.
Branch cracks.
Family plot.

II
Deep-Rooted

Family tree.
Storms blow.
Still standing.

III
Unseasonal

Family tree.
Always spring.
Always fall.

A Coming

IN A KINGDOM WITHIN THE CLOUDS, there lived a plain fairy. The feeling among the fairy people was that she was too plain to be a fairy. Nothing was known of her parentage, though there were rumors about a rakish troll who had breezed through Fairyland not long before the little fairy was seen. Several unusual confluences appeared in the heavens. Observatories on Earth reported an entire distant galaxy swallowed by an incomprehensibly powerful black hole. A star shower blazed across space for a decade, then vanished overnight. Solar flares many times the size of Jupiter erupted, scorching Mercury, yet never so much as blistering our planet.

The immortals of Fairyland, however, had grown blasé about such phenomena over countless millennia. They were more inclined to gossip about the plain little fairy. Fairies are usually goodlooking, and it concerned them that she lowered their Aggregated Good Looks Index.

"I feel for the poor thing," said one fairy, whose wings sparkled like rain. "Her wings are as drab as a sparrow's."

"I know," said another who was constantly courted by fairy princes. "So gray. And that bumpy nose, and oh those crooked teeth. Thank goodness she doesn't smile much."

And, in fact, the plain fairy found little to smile about, except when she was on her own. When she overheard the other fairies, she left quietly, her eyes filling up, eyes the color of mud, lacking the long, silken eyelashes a fairy ought to have. So she fluttered her wings and flew off through the clouds. Then things tended to get better. Her wings, though gray, thrummed a hummingbird's song, and she turned ringsized somersaults or leapfrogged clouds that even the giants of Greatland would have been hardpressed to straddle. Sometimes, when an alpine swift soared by on brown wings, a muddy necklace of feathers across his snowy breast, she hitched a ride on his forehead, lulled by the whoosh of his wings, braced by sky breezes that caught her dark hair. She smiled then, for there was no one to comment on the unevenness of her teeth.

In this manner, she grew to be a very shy adult fairy. The century she stopped growing older—for the fairies were made immortal by Xe From Whom All Springs—she was permitted by Fairyland's Missions Committee to visit our world incognito. On earth, of course, fairies can take any shape, but there are rules. So, while tempted to go as a beautiful girl, she disguised herself as a tiny fly on the wall. Even before there were walls, this was the form taken by observerfairies. Before our time, the disguise worked perfectly; dinosaurs and mastodons could hardly see such an insignificant creature. What better way to observe than be a fly on the wall, we say now and don't know how right we are.

Unfortunately, our plain young fairy chose some grimy walls to settle on, and was shocked by the commonplace things she saw us do. She watched a man murder his brother and another rape his sister, and almost fainted off the face of their walls. She saw squalor and misery in our slums, greed and treachery in corporate boardrooms. So she cut short her visit to a decade. That was long enough to see wars flare up, plagues spread, and species die out. It was a wonder real flies weren't extinct, considering the number of times someone swung a swatter, only to have it pass right through her as she buzzed away.

When she returned to the fairy kingdom she felt an enormous relief, and the unfriendliness of other fairies bothered her less.

"It's such a small thing," she said to herself. "Why complain?"

So she went about her business determined to be content. This was a good thing because, being so plain, she was passed over by fairy gentlemen looking for love. The royal princes and princesses, of whom there were hundreds, had a good time deciding whom to love among scores of beautiful fairies. But the plain fairy was never one of them. In spite of herself, she felt a pang at the sight of fairy couples holding hands, butterflies flitting through puffy clouds. What good is immortal life, she wondered, if I must spend it alone?

ONCE SHE CAME OF AGE, she went down to Earth on fairy missions. At first the Missions Committee entrusted her with minor assignments. Her bleak experience made her dread such returns to the lower world, but she wanted to help. So though her Junior Emissary powers were limited, she found ways to step into areas best left to the committee or to Xe Who Sits Above All.

Nevertheless, she did well enough to be sent on more missions. Her fourth assignment was a tricky future adjustment. It was her first venture into the mind of a human, so she was excited. A twelve-year-old boy had planned a prank on his science teacher that would prompt the poor man to quit. Job-satisfaction suffers when one's shoes are burnt through to the feet by hydrochloric acid beneath the desk. Her job was to proactively remove that plan, by means of her Junior Model wand, from the boy's mind.

When she settled on the prankster's bedroom wall, he was asleep. Dark curls ringed a fresh and innocent face; a smile pulled at the corners of his mouth. Following the instructions in her missions manual, she shrank herself, down, down, down, until she was invisibly small.

As soon as she stepped inside that angelic head, she sank into an oozing mass of pink slime. Horrified, she picked her way along, holding her bumpy nose against the odious stench. The stuff clutched and stuck to her. Wand in hand, she waved it off. Steamy gray vapors lifted from the swamp, singeing her gray wings. Monstrous, splotched toadstools stood all around on twisted stalks. Here and there, a blue lotus struggled to stay afloat, seeming to shrink and close by the moment. One sank with a gurgle. Two tears welled from the plain fairy's eyes. Where they fell, there sprang up two velvety lotuses. She longed to stay and protect them, but she pressed on.

Soon there loomed a particularly malevolent toadstool, larger and more twisted than the rest. By its size and nature she knew it to be her goal. Dwarfed by its swaying fleshiness as she raised her wand, her eyes fell on the very sourcespring of the vile pink substance. It bubbled up in a thick crimson column that boiled over, snarling, into the venomous swamp. And the plain fairy was struck by an idea.

"I wonder," she said aloud, and her words echoed—wonder, under, under—so she went on quietly to herself: I wonder if I couldn't cleanse the source itself.

She decided to try and approached the foul spring with some trepidation. Swinging her wand with all the strength of her tiny arm, she sent a violet stream of stardust pulsing toward the spring. Was it her imagination, or had the bloody root grown a shade lighter? Sensing a change, she launched an assault.

A thousand passes later, she stood swaying, her arm aching, but the slime had turned to spring water, and the source shimmered like champagne. Its spray wetted her lips with glittering beads. Laughing, she splashed into it as the toadstools melted, then slumped and dissolved. The sweet flowing water revived the lotuses so they spread their velvet petals and began to multiply.

Emerging from the boy's head to look once more on that beautiful face, she pondered a moment, then flew back to the fairy kingdom. A deep satisfaction engulfed her and permeated her report to the Missions Committee.

"Maybe," she said to herself, "they'll commend me for my work."

AND BEFORE LONG SHE RECEIVED A SUMMONS from the committee. Now, at the head of every fairy committee are their highnesses, the king and queen of Fairyland. This meant a trip to the fabulous royal palace for the plain fairy. On arriving, she gasped. Towers of smoky topaz caught the sun and turned a thousand colors. Around them rippled a lake of wildflower blue. She crossed the ebony drawbridge just to do things right, for, as we know, fairies can walk on water.

Inside, mothero'pearl flyways teemed with fairy officials going about their business. In awe she drifted around crystal fountains toward the enormous royal hall, where she was ushered into the presence of the king and queen. As befitted their station, they were a tremendously handsome couple. The rest of the committee sat in a semicircle below the emerald thrones, before an audience of royal sons and daughters.

Among them was one of the younger princes, about the age of the plain fairy. He was roughly threehundredth in line to the throne, which obviously didn't mean much. But even being crown princess didn't mean a lot, considering the royal couple is immortal. In any case, it's always nice to be a prince. And he had already begun to display a broader awareness than his brothers and sisters. He was a particularly handsome young prince who had courted many beautiful fairy girls, yet none had tempted him enough to settle down. So he looked curiously at the plain fairy as she stepped, trembling, before his parents. How very plain she is, he thought, and how shy and nervous.

The king addressed the plain fairy. "How are you, my dear?" he asked, nodding as she curtsied before them.

Her voice shook from stagefright. "Very well, your highness."

"Good. We asked you here to review your recent mission, so you might benefit from our thoughts. Most importantly, had you not thwarted that young scoundrel in his plan, his remarkable teacher would have taught no more. But now he will teach all his life. Seven short years from today, he will inspire a student to master nuclear physics. Using simple seawater, she will achieve cold fusion, solving the energy-related problems of the lower world."

The plain fairy ducked her head, thrilled to learn the significance of her completed mission. A flush of gratification surged through her and tinged her dusky wings with color.

"You did creditably, my dear." It was the magnificently robed queen who spoke. "However, being young and inexperienced, you were over-enthusiastic. By making a good person of one intended to be wicked, you altered the course of lowerworld history in a way we hadn't planned. The boy you transformed would have gone on to be a ruthless murderer, and a very useful one indeed. His intended victim will now survive to father a boy—a son who was never meant to be. But as you know, we limit our interventions on Earth, so we will not meddle again. When grown, this son will unwittingly trigger a radiation leak at the last hotfission reactor, resulting in the death and crippling of a million forms of life. Things will not right themselves in that region for generations to come. Human generations, that is."

"Oh!" cried the plain fairy. "I didn't think that the... I didn't mean..."

But her mind whirled with terrible visions of the suffering to come of her good intentions. She fainted and was surrounded by an amazed circle of fairies, all abuzz.

"Treat her gently; let her rest," commanded the queen, who could only pierce the fog of earthly time and was a trifle taken aback by the turn of events. "I will visit her later. We must proceed, however—so many items on the agenda."

THE FIRST BY THE PLAIN FAIRY'S SIDE was the handsome young prince, whose interest had grown as he watched. He lifted her and took her to an inner sanctum. There he laid her on a couch of bees' fur and waited by her side.

When she awoke and remembered, she put her face in her hands and began to sob so hard that the couch became soggy. The prince was moved. Her heart is as soft as she is plain, he thought.

Aloud he said, "Don't cry, miss. Destiny, I'm told, works in unpredictable ways. You shouldn't blame yourself, for you lacked the committee's overview of earthly matters, and you meant well."

At these kind words the plain fairy looked up for a moment and, of course, fell instantly in love with the handsome stranger.

"Who're you?" she asked between sobs.

"I'm one of the royal sons," he said, and she could see from his shining wings and apparel that it was true. "My mother, the queen, will visit us soon. So compose yourself and dry your eyes."

But her eyes were still wet when the queen came by. On seeing this, the queen said, "Don't disturb yourself overly, my dear. Emotion is a nearsighted weakness. Tears are quite unnecessary and rarely of use. A few millennia from now, you will perceive both effects of your mission to be mere stitches in an endlessly stretching, constantly woven tapestry. What does it matter if one stitch goes left and the other right? Each serves the purpose of a stitch. What matter if one is red and the other green? Both build the spectrum of the cloth spewing forth. What matter if one is long and another short? Both are insignificant in comparison to even a fraction of the tapestry. The next two centuries will see an end to all important consequences of the reactor leak. The energy revolution will have more farreaching ramifications, but only relatively so. Ultimately, the human race shall go the way of the dinosaurs, and we will oversee the follies of their successors. And theirs in turn. And theirs."

"Oh," said the plain fairy, a bit overcome by this vision, too polite and in awe to question her queen's irrefutable logic.

But Xe Who Hears Everything heard this pronouncement by one of Xir earliest creations and was not pleased. *My fairies grow hard and proud*, said Xe; *are they still worthy of immortality?*

And Xe Who Put Time In Motion decreed that fairies would no longer be immortal.

A HAPPY PERIOD BEGAN FOR THE PLAIN FAIRY. The young prince spent his time increasingly with her; they rode the upper winds, sat on clouds, dodged the rain into rainbows. She loved him very much. He filled her mind even during her missions, and she was glad to think soon she would see him again.

The prince liked her tremendously too, though at first he didn't think of it as love. So it was a good thing he didn't hear the court gossip over their companionship. He had never met a fairy as sweet and innocent, and when he was with her his mind was at peace. He found contentment he hadn't known before.

After just a decade with her, a strange thing happened—he ceased to think of her as plain. The bumpiness of her nose seemed a charming way for it to be. And when he looked in those muddy eyes, enchanting lights floated in them. Another decade passed swiftly in her company, and he no longer remembered having ever thought her plain.

"You're beautiful," he said one toasty summer night as they hovered in the glow of a golden full moon. "But I must have told you that a thousand times before."

"No," she said, surprised, "you never have.... Do you really think so?"

"From the moment I first saw you. I'm surprised I never told you."

And he turned to her and kissed her, and the stars winked.

The plain fairy's heart was full. I don't think there can ever have been a fairy as happy as I am, she thought.

The prince was happy too. On his way home, he wondered if they might move in together by the end of the decade, even set a wedding date for the next century. But as he drifted through the courtyards that summer night, he passed a group of courtiers deep in conversation. They didn't notice him and continued to talk.

"What news of the young fool prince who's so taken with the plain fairy?" asked one. And the prince stopped to listen—he hadn't heard of a brother of his courting a plain fairy.

"He still is," said another. "What a strange couple they make, he so handsome and she so plain."

"Which prince is this?" asked a third.

"The onehundredandthirtysixth, I believe," replied the second, and the prince stood appalled—they were speaking of him. But what could they mean "so plain"? And a memory began to stir within him.

"Yes," continued the speaker. "One expects better judgment of a royal son."

"I know," said the first. "Bad enough she lowers our AGLI, but now the Royal AGLI may suffer! It's a shame."

The young prince had heard enough and proceeded toward the palace in a doubtridden frame of mind. Ahead of him he saw his parents, the king and queen, taking a walk through the royal garden. Its blooms lit the summer night: morningglory purple, aster blue, violet yellow, gentian red. Their fragrances hung forever in the air, warm and heady, and they washed through the prince's mind whispering strange things. As he was about to hail their royal highnesses, a piece of their conversation floated to him.

"I'm a little worried about our onehundredandthirtysixth son, my dear," said the queen, who, the prince knew, found time to worry about *all* her four hundred and seventy children. "Do you think it's natural he's so interested in that plain little fairy girl of his?"

"Why, what do you mean?" The king tossed his diamond scepter adroitly from his right hand to the left and back again so it reflected the garden colors, a tiny rainbow that skipped through the dark in front of the prince.

"Oh, just that he's so handsome, as befits a son of ours, and she—well, I don't mean to be unkind, but she *is* amazingly plain."

"Yes, well, I wouldn't worry about it, my love. With all the pretty fairies around the palace—not that I notice them, you're so beautiful—but one of them is bound to catch his eye sometime."

"Hmm, yes. Maybe you're right." She reached out to pat him on the cheek and took a quick step back. "Do you know, the moonlight plays strange tricks at times: I almost thought I saw some gray in your hair just then. How absurd!"

And they moved along, leaving the utterly confused prince to sink onto an orange bank of grass.

THAT NIGHT, THOUGH COOLED BY the palace conditioning, the prince shifted restlessly on his bed of cloud. He couldn't shut his eyes without seeing the plain fairy's face in all its onceagain-apparent plainness. When at last he slept, it was in snatches. The slightest whistle of air through the window startled him from dim yet ominous dreams.

The next morning he arose and stood before his raindrop mirror. An elegant image looked back at him, and he couldn't help but agree he was a very goodlooking fairy. His parents and the other fairies were right. That wellbred figure needed an equally attractive consort. No sooner did he think this than the sad face of the plain fairy seemed to peep out from the mirror. But turning away, he made up his mind.

The plain fairy, of course, awoke delirious with joy. The prince's voice echoed in her ears. "You're beautiful," it said. "You're beautiful."

"Maybe I am," she said pertly, unusually at ease with herself, "and maybe not. But I'm glad you think I am."

She wondered how things might change for them now. Would they have sex? What would that be like? Would he wish she were more experienced? Enthralled, she sat in wait for him.

When he came at last, on dazzling wings, she gave him her sweetest smile. But it only showed off her crooked teeth, and he settled on the cloud at a slight distance from her.

How strange, she thought, he always sits by my side; maybe he didn't sleep too well. But the prince assured her he had never slept better.

"Me neither," she said. "I dreamed of you all night, and of what you said."

"Oh, yes," he replied, and a nervous laugh escaped him. "Well, you know how the moonlight affects us all sometimes."

"Oh," she said, the air going out of her. "Then you don't really...?"
And she stopped in confusion.
"Well..." The prince coughed and laughed nervously again.

He didn't mean it, she thought. And she turned away as her eyes filled up. But they refused to clear and the prince said nothing, so she flew blindly away.

FOR THE NEXT THREE DECADES, THE PLAIN FAIRY cried night and day over the fickle prince. She cried alone and she cried in company. She couldn't stop crying when she spoke, no matter what the conversation. She cried as she ate. She cried in her sleep. She cried in all her dreams. She couldn't stop crying even while on her missions. The oppressive sadness of the human condition overwhelmed her with tears. She cried on our walls. She cried inside our heads. She cried for the poor, the fallen, the lost, the feeble, the sick, the dead. She cried for those left behind.

Eventually, she was no longer considered a novice. The committee entrusted her with increasingly difficult tasks requiring ever better judgment, and one by one she discharged them perfectly. So astute did she become in emissary procedure that her recommendations were added to the missions manual. She began to be known for wisdom beyond her youth. Even the prince, who returned half-heartedly to the courtly life, heard of her achievements and felt a mixture of pride and regret.

Down on Earth, too, word spread of miraculous events. Mount Fujiyama, dormant for centuries, belched a creamy load of lava with remarkable healing powers over third-degree burns. A search party from the Alpine town of Brennan swore they were guided over snow-covered slopes by a common housefly, to where a teenage skier lay unconscious with a broken leg. The prayers of a nation were answered when Namibia's aging prime minister sat up on her deathbed, brushed aside her cardiologists' objections, and strode into her central office to enact a historic series of legislations. In hushed discussions everywhere, talk arose of a messiah who would one day save the world.

The plain fairy didn't hear this rumor. She finally stopped crying. She spent the next decades in solitude, except for frequent, bracing rides on her friends the swifts. But she never cried again. It was as if, across three decades of nonstop crying, she'd used up her entire quota of tears. Instead, she found solace in thought. And a calm acceptance came over her.

At the end of seven such decades, she flew into the fairy kingdom to find it abuzz and a strange mood in the air. She passed a fairy gentleman drifting aimlessly, peering into a dewdrop, examining his hair from every angle and tugging at it. Many of the strands were white, a hair-color she had never seen before on fairies. His face was tired; its features sagged as on humans she recalled. She felt compelled to stop him and ask if something was wrong.

"Haven't you heard?" he replied. "The king and queen and older courtiers are showing physical signs of age—wrinkles, graying hair, even their *wings* have started to shrivel. At first, we were enormously concerned about the effect on our AGLI. But now it's happening to us, too, and it's clear there are even grimmer implications. We are no longer immortal; that's what it means. We shall all, in time, grow old and perish."

The plain fairy tried to think of something comforting to say, but he had rushed on already, and was part of a heated discussion in a group of gesticulating fairies. It's a good thing, she thought, they aren't holding their wands—who knows what would happen down on Earth? Her own hands, she noticed, turning them over, seemed a bit weathered. She looked around and saw groups of agitated fairies. Here and there, bedraggled middle-aged ladies wept into chrysalis silk handkerchiefs. Their wings drooped. Comparatively young ladies and gentlemen were rendered unattractive by the disgust on their faces. Fairy youths flitted around, laughing, chattering, and pointing at less fortunate others. The little children just looked confused.

Still tearless from the strength she had found over a century of contemplation, the plain fairy turned sadly away and flew to her secluded cloud at the edge of Fairyland. *I wish,* she thought with all her might, *there were something I could do!*

And at last Xe Who Dwells Deep Within Our Minds spoke through hers. *My child,* Xe said, *there is a way, but it is hard.*

She looked around in confusion. "Who was that?" she asked.

Xe who caused the stars to burn, said the great androgynous voice, *Xe who makes the mountains rise and the thistle grow. I gave the turtle her shell, the fox his tail. I gave you your wings.*

"Oh?" said the plain fairy. "Then if you are the cause of all the grief I see around me, it's no wonder you don't show your face."

A sound of laughter boomed in her head, and Xe said, *You have seen me before, and you will see me again.*

"Don't talk in riddles," said the plain fairy sternly. "Reveal yourself or leave me alone."

Look, then, said Xe; *look upon my face.*

And the heavens turned dark. Rain fell in torrents, and the wind came howling through trees that sprang out of nowhere, a forest in the sky. Lightning gored the earth, and light and darkness played across the plain fairy's face as she looked on in fright. The forest swayed and creaked, swayed and creaked beneath an avalanche of water.

A great crack of thunder broke across the landscape, and it seemed to say: *I am Chance.*

"Yes," said the plain fairy in a subdued voice. "Yes, I see."

And soft laughter sounded in her head. The sun came out from behind clouds to send luminous rays over treetops greener than the royal thrones. Birds twittered and flapped in a hundred different plumages, and the clouds cleared to reveal a blue that had been there forever.

A light breeze smelling of mist lifted strands of her hair and whispered: *I am Order.*

"Yes," she said, smiling and shaking her head where the breeze tickled her. "I can see that quite clearly."

Then the twittering grew, and an alpine swift streaked from a hill on long pointed wings curved like a bow. It dashed toward her at breakneck speed as she wondered if she might hitch a ride to think of what she had seen. But it bore up at her, larger every second, until it was all bristles and fierce, beady eyes above a beak that disclosed a cavernous maw. She hung frozen in place, about to be swallowed. But it whooshed by at the final instant, sending her spinning, and the beak closed with a mighty snap around a hapless bug.

Then the great bird balled up in the sky above her, its animal smells overpowering, uttering shrill, exultant cries that drowned the sound of her heart. And it seemed to shriek: *I am Instinct.*

"Yes," she admitted, putting her hands over her ears. "I see you are."

At which the hovering ball of feathers melted like candlewax and ballooned into the head of a sleeping child. So blameless and unblemished was the giant face floating above her that she recognized the young prankster whose mind she had once visited. Dark eyelashes many yards long rested on full, rosy cheeks, and warm breath issued rhythmically between parted lips, wrapping her in fog. The eyelashes lifted to reveal piercingly bright eyes. The lips moved, sending air currents swirling around her, and a breaking voice said: *I am Consciousness.*

"Yes," she agreed hesitantly. "You are, but...but of toadstools or lotuses?"

The laughter boomed again, and the face shifted into the long, brooding features of the man she had once seen murder his brother. He sneered down at her as she shrank from him. Rapidly the head changed again, and from it gazed the dulleyed countenance of the woman raped by her brother. As the plain fairy gasped, it turned swiftly into the weak features of the young prince smiling uncertainly at her. She wondered if she ought to smile back, but the giant face was changing again, and to her astonishment she found herself staring at an enormous bumpy nose and huge brown eyes above a gentle mouth that smiled quietly, showing a range of crooked teeth like hills.

Then the face and the forest in the sky were gone, and the plain fairy found herself seated on the cloud by herself again, with only the voice of Xe Who Is The Great Universe for company.

And Xe Who Is Truth said: *Had you seen me before, my child?*

"I had," she replied humbly, quite overcome, looking earnestly into the emptiness as if she could still see Xe in all Xir incomprehensible greatness. But there was only cloud swirling in myriad particles that enveloped her and contained her, seemed to flow into and out of her in promise of eternal assimilation.

"You must forgive me for being so rude at first," she continued. "It's not really like me. But I was so worried about my people...."

Undoubtedly, said Xe Who Understands Everything. *And again I say: there is a way to help them, but it is hard.*

"What way is that?" she asked without hesitation.

Should a fairy wholly innocent of pride, said Xe Who Is Beyond Time, *surrender her fairy privilege to be reborn a human, her sacrifice would restore the natural balance. And the fairies would be immortal again.*

At this, an old fear took hold of the plain fairy with all its terrible strength, and she said quietly, "I don't mind being mortal, but I fear the things humans do. Even more, I fear what *I* might do, once human."

My child, said Xe Who Is Wisdom Itself, *you have seen my many faces.*

The plain fairy didn't quite follow, but her mind swept back to the different faces of Xe. Great toadstools in a pink swamp sprang up before her eyes. They blocked out the sun, and she dropped into shadow.

When she awoke, rocked gently on the cloud, she remembered with less dread the answer to her wishes. Thoughts of her people came back to her—the mothers and fathers and children of Fairyland, and even the prince she couldn't forget. Creeping behind came the question: why sacrifice herself for those who had spurned her? But she put it away, and at the thought of saving the children, her acceptance grew. I'm only one, she reflected, while they are so many.

At which she sprang to her feet. The strength of giants filled her, and her voice rolled across the clouds, bold and rich as never before.

"I'm ready," she cried. "Send me down!"

AS STRANGELY AS IT HAD BEGUN, THE AGING of the fairies ceased. No one knew how to explain either event, but they were tremendously relieved—all except the crown princess, who had hoped finally to be queen. Many were chastened, though, by the much older appearance they would now have to live with forever. And, of course, nobody missed the plain fairy. When called upon for her next mission, she was found to have vanished. The feeling among those still young enough was, Well, how strange, but it certainly raises our AGLI. They were only able to say that for a short while. The king and queen had already aged so much that, with their shriveled wings and parchment skin, they were no longer as goodlooking as even the commoners. That was an absurd state of affairs, so they banned further calculation of the AGLI.

No, nobody missed the plain fairy. Except the now older prince. For some reason, even in the lively company of the most beautiful fairies, he found himself still thinking of her. He wondered where she might have gone. Sometimes he flew to their old cloud and sat there by himself, lost in thought. One day he noticed two small objects that stuck, fluttering, out of a fold of cloud. The sight provoked a strange, uneasy feeling, and on drifting over he saw them to be a pair of musty gray wings.

No one has any knowledge of those first days, unless he has heard tales
passed down from father to son.

— Abolqasem Ferdowsi, Shahnameh: The Persian Book of Kings

And the first gray of morning fill'd the east,
And the fog rose out of the Oxus stream.

— Matthew Arnold, "Sohrab and Rustum"

The Legend of Rostam and Sohrab

The Singer, I

COME CLOSER. LEAVE YOUR FLOCKS A WHILE. Shed your fleece—the fire will warm you. Call your beloved and your children to hear my song. Carry your aged and infirm. I will sing to you all.

My song is the song of Persia, may we prosper under Kai Kusru. I sing of our vast and spreading land, from the seashore of Pars to the plains of Khorasan to the Alborz Mountains to the Oxus River. I sing of our warriors, their beloveds, their bloodlines. I sing of their battles, their foes. I sing of the fallen, may the light of Ohrmuzd shine upon them. They gilded the land with our banner 'til they could hoist it no more. Then they reddened the ground with their blood.

My voice is the low drum of war-weary Rostam, warrior of warriors, spearhead of Persia, champion of kings. It is the nightingale's trill of his forbidden love, the Turkish princess Tahmina. It is the young lion's roar of Sohrab, who knew not his father but vowed to seek him on the battlefield.

Have all assembled around the fire? Hush, then. Listen.

Chapter 1
Sohrab Investigates the Mystery of His Birth

MY PEOPLE THINK I HAVE EVERYTHING. I am heir to the throne of Samangan: my grandfather is the shah, my mother is Princess Tahmina. Of age at last, I tower many hands over other young Turks. My arms are as their thighs, my thighs as their waists. None can best me at the royal polo, as long as there's a horse that can heft me. When we hunt, my falcon inevitably tastes blood at the tips of my arrows and my javelin. As for weapons of war: the iron maces, spears, scimitars, and shields are like toys in my hands. I must hold back or risk wounding my dueling partners. When we wrestle, I toss sturdy pehlvans around like children.

I live in luxury. Put it this way: I live in a palace. The palace attendants wait on me hand and foot if I don't dismiss them. I dismiss them. Better a warrior than a pampered prince. But the former needs food as much as the latter. More. I love to eat. I stuff my mouth with stuffed dolma and sluice them down with sherbet and wine. My name breaks down to Red Shining Water, after all: my mother says I came into the world red in the face. Then bring on the kebabs, drown the trout in tartar sauce, and serve the pilav with lamb, curd, and pistachio as do our Persian enemies. I was never above that. And don't skip the sugared halva. Not so long ago, I thought it was my appetite that had grown me so big.

Do the women like me? What do you think? Ours is a land of sensual music, vibrant dance, undulating hips, passionate women. But I don't make an ass of myself. A prince must be discreet with the occasional friend, or his people will talk. And I don't need to be the subject of more gossip—it's the fishbone in my tartar sauce. Not all my people place me on a pedestal. To some I'm not the prince but—let me say it plainly—the royal bastard.

So I *don't* have everything—far from it. Specifically, I have no known father. I grew up without one. My grandfather is a great man and a doting grandparent, but he is not a father: too old for that, and too steeped in matters of state. His nephew Zhende Razm, my mother's cousin, has been a fond uncle to me. He grooms me for the throne. My mother, ah, no child could have had a gentler mother, and no man in all the land one prouder of him. But a mother cannot be a father. Mother was wise not to try. What good would it have done for a beautiful, sophisticated woman to shed embroidered silks for a rough hunting habit, let alone scour the scrubby hills for wild ass and boar?

I don't mean I was left wanting for hunting companions or tutelage. Nor do I speak only of fatherly guidance. No, it's a missing feeling, the absence of which haunts my every moment, sleeping and waking. Not a feeling I can describe, never having known it, but its utter absence is a void that physically aches. As for mentally, my mother was ever aware of my dark moods, even as I sensed the sadness that periodically enveloped her. Neither of us needed to ask the other why.

Yet she had the advantage of me, for she knew exactly what and whom she missed, having had both before losing them. And she refused to tell me. No one else could: not even my grandfather or uncle knew, or so they said. I'd ask her over and over—ever since I noticed other children with not one but two parents—only to hear this: "Life of my life, blood of my blood, one day I will tell you, but not now. One day I will no longer have a dearest boy, for he will be a man. When I see before me that dearest young man, ask me then."

With that, she'd try to pull me to her perfumed robes, but I'd stalk off, swinging at Chinese vases and other breakables. Many a wrestling playmate felt the burgeoning heft of my holds, many a wild onager the sting of my arrows, many a dueling partner the swift surge of my Indian blade.

But I grew toward that day.

AT LAST, I STOPPED GROWING SKYWARD and added only girth. So much that the polo horses buckled under my weight. One day on the field, as hawks sailed across a blazing sky and great drops of sweat splashed off me, I reined my laboring steed to the side and beckoned my uncle. Tugging his reins he came over, a formidable figure though three-quarters my size. My mother and he share the deep affection that cousins without siblings have for each other, and he regards me as a full nephew.

"Oho, young man," he called out. "Your horse *and* your team are stumbling. Concede."

I nodded tolerantly as his horse trotted up and settled. "Zhende bey," I said, "I give a damn about games anymore. So let's say you win. But the polo field is one thing, the battlefield another. I couldn't afford to be on a lame little pony there."

Behind his salted beard, my uncle's expression seemed to sober. "Well, we're not at war, but let's find a warhorse worthy of you."

"Good! Thanks." I felt the war lust mount in me. "*You've* been in battles."

"Yes." Now there was no question about his change of mood. "I rode on Afrasiab's second campaign against Iran. Not long before you were born."

Afrasiab, commander of the Turanian army back then, is now king of Turan. He eliminated his princely competition by hacking his own brother in two. So much for sibling affection. The departed prince had even bigger problems than mine. Looking at it another way, he has none now. And at least he knew his father, Shah Pashang.

"Speaking of my birth, what did you call me as you came over?"

"Uh, 'young man?' Haven't I called you that before?"

"You have. You have. But are you starting to mean it?"

"Let me think…." He pursed his lips, then smiled at my sardonic reaction. "Starting. Yes, starting to mean it. But why the rush? There's plenty of time."

"You sound like my mother when she puts off my inquiries," I said, my own mood souring. "Today she will not. The time has come. See to the matter of my steed, dear uncle. I go to her courthouse."

Chapter 2
Tahmina Sees Her Dearest Young Man

THE DAY I DREADED YET LONGED FOR HAS COME. As I lounged

this morning on my plump sequined pillows, one of my younger attendants coyly drew her veil while another giggled and fiddled with her wavy black hair. I sat up at once, knowing which visitor was their target. Ceremoniously an older attendant sprayed a cloud of fragrant rosewater in the air, and into it strode my young giant of a son. Disgustedly waving aside the perfume, he pulled himself up to his great height so that it sank beneath his griffon nose. As always now when faced with his adult enormity, I have to remind myself that he'd once fitted in my womb—less and less well as my term wore on, but encased within me nonetheless.

Switching to a more agreeable expression he said, "Ladies, it grieves me to lose your company as soon as I've found it, but I must request private audience with the princess."

A dormant sense of foreboding rose from my chest to render me light-headed. A hand to the giving pillows failed to steady me. Amid teasing protests from the women, I dismissed them.

"Life of my life," I said with a tremor in my voice, "I am indisposed today—something sits on my chest. The sight of you lifts it, but these private sessions of ours are so distressing."

"Mutually so, Mother," he said gruffly, his expression souring again. "That 'something' has sat on your chest since before I was born. It's about time we got it off—take a good look at your grown son and deliver on your promise."

"My love," I ventured, "that you are now admittedly enormous in body does not mean it is yet matched by your wisdom. I fear you are not ready to know everything. Your youthful impatience still tells me so."

"I see," he said. "So my impatience has everything to do with my never-ending 'youth' and nothing to do with your willfully withholding the origin of my life for, let me see, all my damned life! I'm in awe of *your* wisdom, Mother."

I sighed. "Well, maybe sarcasm is a sign of impending maturity, though I do not appreciate it when directed at me by my own son. Let me think upon this. Try me again when the summer heat no longer enervates me."

And I gestured him away with a hand that peeked out from under a silver-threaded sleeve.

But he tensed beneath his sweaty polo attire. "Mother, you are incomparably dear to me, so I give you fair warning. Do *not* test my alleged impatience any further." Even clearer warning was the anger flooding his beautiful young face. "If you think this time I will stop at rearranging your interior décor, you're wrong. I swear to you the first man I encounter outside your lifelong retreat from reality will have his *bones* rearranged to bear witness to his prince's manhood."

"Sohrab!" I cried, hastily making room for him on my pillows and patting the spot. "Do not dare lay your oversized hands on my good men. Is that your measure of manhood, your ability to dismember a fellow man?"

Still disgruntled but quickly picking up on my implication, he settled his bulk by my side. "Aha. So at last you acknowledge that I am now a man among fellow men. Thank you. Now, finally, make good on your interminable promise."

There was no escaping it any longer, and dark foreboding filled me like water boiling up in a covered pot. "So I must, it seems. But first consider this vanishing moment. Remember the fortunate life you—we—have led and that what I tell you might change it forever. Now: do you still wish to hear the story?"

I looked up into my son's eyes and saw in them the rush of unutterable relief. I had my answer before he spoke, his voice now gentle and sad. "Mother, you did not raise a thankless fool. Yes, I've had a remarkably fortunate existence. Most men would unhesitatingly swap places with a prince. But most men have had fathers. Most men have not always had to wonder who their father was, where he was, what he was, how he was.... I may have lived the good life, but it has not been an entirely happy one. And forgive me for insisting, but I don't think yours has been, either."

I dropped my eyes as they started to fill. Then as I'd done for so long, I held the tears back, and when at last I began my voice was steady.

Chapter 3
Tahmina Tells Sohrab of Rostam

VERY WELL, THEN. IMAGINE, IF YOU CAN, your mother a young woman. Yes: I was young woman first, princess second. And like any young woman, I dreamed of a remarkable man. But unlike your playboy lifestyle— oh yes, I've heard of your women, so don't bother denying it—mine was a secluded life. A princess cannot make free of herself without generating tremendous scandal. Your grandfather was accordingly protective and kept me indoors. Few men saw what the attendants said was my beautiful face.

Then one day, I heard them chattering at a higher pitch than usual. Naturally, I demanded to know what the gossip was about. Their unofficial leader Seda—yes, the very Seda, my senior attendant, who receives you with rosewater—young and comely in those days, Seda was already bursting to tell me.

"Princess, as day broke and our sentries changed place, pacing angrily up the palace road with a saddle slung over his massive shoulder came a war elephant of a man. 'Is this,' he bellowed, 'a kingdom of horse thieves? Who dares steal the fabled Raksh from Rostam as he sleeps?' Upon which, one of the guards scrambled to inform your father that the great Persian warrior Rostam was in Samangan on a hunt. Well, the shah came below to personally assure him that Raksh and his abductors would be tracked down. And while that was done, Rostam would be our honored guest."

"Oh?" I said casually, though of course I'd heard of the Iranian warrior who'd bested our commander Afrasiab in man-to-man combat and ended his invasion of Iran. "So this foreigner is to stay in the palace until then?"

"Yes," she said, smiling slyly. "And I happen to know in which guest chamber. So though one stallion is lost, maybe another has been found."

"That's disgusting, Seda. At least try not to mix your animal metaphors. Is this…this Rostam a towering elephant *and* a bellowing bull *and* a stallion in bed?"

"That's for you to find out."

I rolled my eyes.

"Tahmina, listen to me. How often have you bemoaned the scarcity of suitable or even just taller men? Rare beauty though you are, you know you're no petite little thing. Then right to your door comes this legendary warrior who, at the very least, is several hands taller, yet you turn up your pretty nose at him without a single look?"

Well, she had a point.

So that night I followed Seda, a fragrant ambergris candle in her hand, to the stranger's room. The candle's glow lit the hushed corridors only a short, flickering distance. In its light and shade, my embroidered royal robe shifted color.

"O great warrior from afar," she said softly at the entrance. "May we have audience with you?"

A moment of silence, then a muffled yet bone-deep voice: "May I know who requests it?"

"My lady Tahmina, the Princess of Samangan."

Sounds of hurried motion. The curtain was swept aside to reveal a bearded colossus. Bushy eyebrows raised, he ushered us in and gestured toward sequined cushions reflecting candlelight.

When I made no move toward them, he too stayed on his feet. His eyes, as dark as caves, appraised me too directly, so I sent mine around the chamber, taking in his quiver of hunting arrows, his heavy mace, and the sheathed sweep of his sword.

Seda, never shy, cried out: "Is that the mace with which you crushed the head of a war elephant?"

His eyes finally left my face, as if grudgingly. "Yes. It grieved me to kill the rampaging beast, but it had trampled dozens of warriors to death."

I, always shy with men, was inspired by that to speak. "You see, O Rostam, that word of your legendary feats reached us long before you did."

"Princess Tahmina," he replied, "the subject of legends rarely lives up to them. But the legend of your great beauty did not—could not—convey the reality before me now. And so sweet is your voice it renders this rough warrior speechless."

I smiled my reward at him. "You do very well, for a speechless man."

Seda giggled, reminding me we were not alone. I turned toward her. "Seda, you may leave us now, thanks."

Even someone as forward as Seda was shocked. "My lady, the shah would not wish you to be left unaccompanied…."

"I doubt," I said wryly, "that my father would wish me here at all, even accompanied."

"If he finds out, Tahmina, it will be the end of my days at court. And our guest of honor would find himself no longer the welcome guest."

At that the gruff stranger, now strangely familiar to me, spoke up. "I will gladly risk that, if this is what the princess wishes."

"She does wish."

"In that case," Seda said, shaking her head but putting the candle down to hug me tight, "I will risk it too."

She slipped past the curtain into the dark, and we were free to take each other in without looking away.

"My lady," he said at last. "You honor me beyond words. I cannot repay that by bringing dishonor on you in the eyes of your father, who has been a generous host to me."

I nodded nervously. "He already risks the ire of Afrasiab, whose defeat at your hands will sting him forever. But understand this: good man though my father is, he could never allow us the traditional path. Afrasiab would see that as a public alliance with his greatest enemy and charge my father with treason."

The hooded eyes that had softened so wonderfully as they looked into mine finally fell. "Had I known the eventual cost of humiliating Afrasiab on the battlefield, *I* would have turned tail before he did."

It opened my heart, this proud man's willingness to accept defeat if it meant he could win me. "Then let's not speak of honor and dishonor between us now."

Instinctually, I lifted my royal headdress and put it aside. My black tresses tumbled over my robe in a way no man had seen before.

He understood. Stepping close, he took my hand. It caught fire in his. This time, when he turned toward the cushions, I went with him.

Chapter 4
Sohrab's Plan Frightens Tahmina

"A WEEK LATER," I CONCLUDED, "RAKSH WAS FOUND, and your grandfather ordered the horse-thieves punished. The famous stallion was ceremoniously restored to Rostam, who mounted and waved to the court as he rode off to his land. People said he did not look happy, and they feared he might return with the Iranian army to punish us all. But in truth, his face fell as that parting wave went beyond their heads to me, where I watched from a distance, my face wet with tears. I knew it would be the last time I saw your father."

"My father!" Sohrab roared, face upturned and ablaze. "My father is the legendary Rostam!"

"Shh, lower your voice. Aside from Seda, no one else has ever known. Until you now...."

"Why?" Still loud. "Why withhold it from me? And he the great warrior all along!"

"Exactly why—I knew a young boy could not control his impulse to shout it to the world, until inevitably it reached the ear of Afrasiab. Then you, too, would have been lost to me."

"Afrasiab! My great father gave him the drubbing of his life—he barely escaped with it and would not have dared cross the dreaded Rostam again."

I sighed. "Your father has no idea you even exist. It's safer that way. For both of you."

"Safer? Safer for him to not have the joy of knowing his son? Safer for me to suffer the shame and deprivation of not having a father?"

"Yes. Safer for your grandfather as well. Safer for all of Samangan."

At that reminder, he checked his scowl, hunched his massive shoulders, and stared through my thick Persian carpet as if it were water. I watched him, my heart aching.

At last those distant eyes lifted. "Then I must set out from Samangan to seek my father."

"No!" I cried. "For a Turk to venture into Iran is to court death."

"So it's a good thing it turns out I'm half-Persian. But I will not go alone. With my grandfather's blessing and Zhende Bey's help I shall assemble a great army."

"An army!" I said bitterly. "Your father's war-lust is in you. I suppose it doesn't matter that you don't have your *mother*'s blessing."

"Not unless you could help bring in the recruits. But you *will* bless me when I find my father and unite our families. He'll be overjoyed to know the illustrious line of Saum, Zaul, and Rostam shall not end with him."

"And Afrasiab? Will he be overjoyed to learn this?"

"I'm tired of hearing that name. Let him think my campaign is to expand his kingdom. And expand it I will. But once my father and I join hands—"

"Drop your voice," I hissed. "Drop…your…voice."

He refused to drop it.

"When Rostam and Sohrab march together, our combined army shall sweep everything before it! This time, Afrasiab will fall. Then Iran and Turan will be one."

It was as if all my hidden fears and all my secret hopes were simultaneously coming true.

My voice reflected this ambivalence as I went to my cypress armoire and returned to his side. "Go then, without my blessing, but with this seal of Zaul your father gave me."

The old armband gleamed to see light again as I tied it on him. Its insignia, a golden-beaked griffon with scarlet crest and Persian-blue plumage, pulsed as if alive when Sohrab reverently touched it.

"From his great arm to yours—a perfect fit," I said ruefully. "He will know you by it. And Zhende has seen him twice: on the battlefield and in court. Tell your uncle nothing, but ask him to identify the great Rostam for you. Now may Yazdan guide you and bring you back to me."

And I pulled him tight. For once, he did not pull away. "Not only will I return," he said, quiet at last, "I'll bring my father with me. Your silent parting before I was born shall not be the last you see of him."

I drew back just enough to see my grown son through a screen of unshed tears. "Except for one terribly short week, I've lived without him and survived the pain. But you *are* my life: I would not last without you. So, life of my life, it is my turn to hold you to your word."

He took my hands in his. "I promise."

Then he rose to his feet and strode toward his destiny.

The Singer, II

SO IT WAS THAT THE PRINCE OF SAMANGAN sent forth a call to arms that rang sweetly on the ears of restless young Turks. Zhende Razm brought in the veterans, and their army marched like a giant centipede toward the craggy outposts of Iran. One by one, the smaller fortresses fell before their bloody onslaught. Sohrab's reputation as a fiery young leader and ferocious warrior reached Afrasiab. Pleased, the Shah of Turan sent twelve thousand horsemen under Houman to swell the army. Now it blanketed the mountain passes like a swarm of locusts, 'til at last only a white-stone fortress stood between them and the plains of Khorasan.

From the high fortress walls, its commander surveyed this vast horde camped endlessly along a tributary of the Oxus. Gazhdaham knew his fort could not hold for long. He dispatched a swift rider to carry this message to the Shah of Iran. Horse after horse, the relay galloped through the night, until the exhausted messenger reached the Persian court. As soon as he heard of the powerful young Turk threatening Iran's border, Kai Kaus mobilized the immense Persian army. The din of war-drums, the glint of shields, and the dust of a hundred thousand horsemen filled the air. As the war elephants turned ponderously toward Khorasan, he dispatched the veteran chieftain Gaev to Zabul, where the greatest warrior of all, the graybeard Rostam, had hoped to retire.

Chapter 5
Rostam is Reluctant

FOR AN AGING WARRIOR, RETIREMENT IS DOUBLE-EDGED. I am bone-tired of spilling blood. Yet a life of peace is comparatively dull. Restful, yes. Exciting, no. Days of relaxation stretch into the future, each like the other. So on what seemed just another such day, I left the suffocating walls we build around us, the indulgent cushions into which we sink, the numbing chatter that passes for connection, and rode out with my trusted old friend. Raksh and I *are* connected. We move together. His hooves slash the sands: I feel them. My mood lifts: he feels it.

Eventually we came to the saffron fields, slowed to a canter, and entered a purple-blue world. Raksh picked his way along. Crushed flowers sent up their fragrance, his nostrils flared, and he lowered his great head to graze. I dismounted as lightly as possible for so large a man, yet cropped a flower beneath my sandals. Picking it up, I pushed at the crimson stamens that rose within its petals. When powdered they flavor my pilav. Now they stained my finger a dull yellow. Around it the violet petals bloomed only for this week, and they played with my mind. I'm not the kind to give a woman flowers, but they reminded me of one who'd bloomed so generously for an enemy warrior across just one precious week.

When I think of Tahmina—and I try not to—I think of pointless things. What if I could have stayed on? What if Turan and Iran were not at odds? What if we could have married and raised a family? Boys and girls running around us, all over the grounds. The gentleness of motherhood on Tahmina's face. The pride of fatherhood on mine.

As I stood drowning in what-ifs, Raksh raised his powerful neck and twitched his ears. Then I, too, heard the dull thud of hooves. As the horseman drew nearer, I saw it was my old brother-in-arms, Gaev, sweat pouring off his horse. This was not going to be just another day, after all.

Dismounting hurriedly, he left a trail of trampled flowers as he came at me, calling my name. We embraced, and our horses stretched out their necks to nose at each other.

"Gaev," I said, "much wine has slid down this gullet since last I saw you. You look well. Salted and wiser. I'm still big, but not stupid: I know nothing good could have brought you this far at a gallop. So whatever it is, don't tell me today. Let me give you a taste of the good life, and maybe you'll forget about it and join me in retired amnesia."

"Rostam, old friend, I wish I did not have to disturb the peace you've paid so dearly for with your scars. But I must. Kai Kaus calls urgently on you to rejoin his forces as we make our way as rapidly as we can toward the border."

"Border be damned. I detest the thing. What is it good for? I'll tell you what: keeping people on opposite sides of it. So how does it matter where it lies? Turanians are still going to live on the other side and we're still going to live on this side."

Gaev exhaled noisily. "You know how it is with the shahs. Afrasiab wants rule over more of the land, and Kai Kaus wants rule over more of the land. The last thing he wants is to rule over *less*. Let me restate that: the very last thing he wants is to no longer rule."

"No fear of that. We taught Afrasiab and his warriors a lesson there's not enough wine in the entire land to make them forget."

He nodded. "We did, but the players have changed. I see you haven't heard of Afrasiab's protégé. Quite the new power. Fearless. Bloody. He fights, they say, with boiling anger."

My eyebrows went up. "Ah. Too young to remember their defeats, yet he remembers *something*. I wonder what…. Well, fine, if Kai Kaus is so concerned about this upstart, let him go fight his own wars. I, for once, am just an interested spectator."

"Rostam, Rostam, since when does the shah fight on the frontline?" Then a sly look replaced the exasperation. "Besides, word is he'd be no match for this pehlvan. Word is there may be *no* match for him. He is heads taller than other warriors, twice their girth, and wields his weapons with unparalleled skill and ferocity."

"Unparalleled?" I smiled at his transparent ploy. "In that case, I'd be of no use. Come, let's drink to that, and then you can go tell the shah you found me an aging, drunken, useless wreck."

Gaev gestured apologetically. "It's merely what the youngsters say. I who have seen you loose terror upon enemy ranks tried to describe to them the greatness of Rostam, and of course they've heard of your peerless exploits. But what they have not seen for themselves remains an absent phantom that does not register. I fear that without you there to see, hear, and believe in, they will be demoralized by this bloodthirsty behemoth who has swept all before him."

I could no longer affect a sanguine disregard. "Hmm. Does this monster have a name?"

"Sohrab."

I shifted uneasily, and then so did Raksh. "Red water. Shining. Luminous. Not a monstrous name.... But then, which parents ever saw a future monster when naming their ruddy-faced infant?"

"Monster or not, his forces—and Afrasiab's—are poised to enter and ravage Iran. No man has stood taller in her defense than you have, so it's unfair to ask that you take up arms for her again. But she needs you."

Now, that's another thing about peacetime: if you're not a family man, nobody really needs you.

I considered the lilac tranquility around us. Then feeling a sense of purpose once more in spite of myself, I exhaled. Too damned pretty for an aging warrior anyway. "All right, Gaev. Let's get you a solid meal and a fresh horse. Where along the border are we headed?"

My old friend brightened visibly at having succeeded. Who knew what delights the shah might have ordered for him—and me—had he not. "The white fortress south of the Oxus."

"Ah." A bolt of excitement shot through me. Not all that far from Samangan. Maybe…

Even Raksh pranced like a colt as I mounted.

Chapter 6
Rostam Assesses the Enemy

CARRYING LITTLE AND MOVING FAST, WE CROSSED the vast plains of Khorasan, then circled mountainous Balkh. Bringing our slathered horses to a walk, we found the Iranian army arrayed on one side of the Zibad as it flowed toward the Oxus. Along the opposite bank were lined, as if in a mirror, the forces of Turan. Behind them rose the white walls of our border fortress—ours no more. It had fallen to the Turanian upstart.

"Gazhdaham and his men?" I asked Tus, as Gaev and I devoured welcome offerings, meat-juice greasing our beards. I could hear murmurs from nearby warriors eyeing the roughly attired behemoth who had now joined their force.

He shook his head. "Wiped out. To a man. Had the messenger not made it out in time, Sohrab would be marching toward Isfahan now."

For the first time, like a tide along the Caspian Sea, a great anger rose in me toward this bloody and merciless new foe. The very sound of his name grated on me. It finally struck me that red water is blood.

"Who is this callow upstart?" I barked. "I want to see him for myself—ten to one the reality won't match the myth. Guide me to the nearest crossing point. At dusk I'll slip across and take measure of our bloodthirsty friend."

WHEN YOU'VE BEEN ONLY TOO VISIBLE most of your life, the cloak of dark waters, however chilly, is a comfort. Just the gentle swoosh of water flecked by starlight. I emerged at a short distance from the Tartar camp. To the audible crunch of riverside grit beneath my considerable bulk, I stepped as lightly as I could. The nearer I came, the slower I went. A low buzz around the camp began to cover my footsteps. But no water to cover me now, and less darkness. Staggered campfires gave out a flickering glow that glanced alarmingly off my dagger sheath and dripping apparel.

I circled warily until the largest fire caught my eye. Crouching, I crept closer. Gathered around it, a group of veterans leaned forward to listen intently to a young chieftain, by his almost princely attire. The young fellow evidently liked even his battle uniform the way a peacock likes its feathers: bright and on display. And yet, the older men paid him their full attention. It wasn't hard, even at a distance, to see one reason why. He was gigantic. Other than in pool reflections of myself, I had never seen such a mountainous human. I couldn't hear his words, but his tone and demeanor were supremely confident, bordering on arrogant. That unearned cockiness from such a ruthless young man—for this could only be Sohrab—reignited the deep anger in me. And now it felt personal. There is something about a good-looking face that makes you think you have seen it before, even the very first time you see it. Firelight played across it as he spoke, at times leaving it as dark as his deeds and at times as luminous as his name.

A graybeard by his side, a large man in his own right yet dwarfed by Sohrab, sat back with an indulgent look on his face. As he lifted it to look around, I felt that it too was familiar, but in a different way. I *had* seen it before, probably on a battlefield. A veteran, then, from Afrasiab's campaigns. So that treacherous usurper of Turan's throne was indeed behind this renewed attack and, with the giant Sohrab's help, poised yet again to conquer Iran. And yet again it was not up to Kai Kaus himself but left to the shah's old guard, that old reliable, Rostam, to put his life on the line and the enemy to flight. Of course. Except that the enemy was as large as Rostam this time, and now Rostam was old.

As this mishmash of anger, resentment, and weariness of it all roiled within me, I kept my eyes on the alert veteran. Presumably a senior advisor, going by his position at Sohrab's side and his stately apparel. Then in display of a phenomenon that I've observed before yet always surprises me, some telepathic or other sense brought his roving eyes around to the peripheral shadows where I sat, trying to look casual. Well, one can disguise intention, but there's no disguising enormity. He rose quietly from the campfire and, affecting disinterest himself, drifted in my general direction.

Canny veteran that he was, he kept his eyes mostly averted. Canny veteran myself, I took the opportunity to shift back toward the dark. But he kept coming. The closer he came, the more uneasy I grew. The more tense I felt, the more casually I reclined. The more unconcerned I looked, the closer he came without feeling the need to sound an alarm. That was the bigger danger, the one to prevent at all cost. The old buzz in my head and tingling of limbs in time of danger was building. Toward a bursting point. By now he was close enough that some form of encounter seemed certain. And I began to measure the narrowing gap in terms of my giant reach. I could not afford to let him get inside of it. So I readied my muscles. And watched. And waited.

Then he was openly approaching to ask who I was, and things happened quickly. I rose to my feet, towering above him. His eyes traveled the tree trunk of my body to my face. And opened wide in the unmistakable look of recognition. I still couldn't tell who he was, but he knew exactly who *I* was. That doomed him. Before his mouth could open further, my knife was out of its sheath and, in the same motion, slashing hard across his throat. He gurgled blood as it bubbled out, his eyes rolled upward, and I caught him as he crumpled.

Lowering him carefully to the ground, I watched the lifeblood flow out of him. My head felt clogged. Years had passed since my last kill. And I'd truly believed that phase of my life was over. Eventually I closed the warrior's eyelids forever, and retreated into the night.

THE STREAM WAS COLDER ON THE WAY BACK. A dense fog rolled around me as I swam. I let a shiver subside before going cautiously into camp to join Gaev and Tus around our own crackling central fire. Warming my hands over it, breathing its acrid fumes, I took their questions.

"You don't look happy," Tus said.

"I'm not. On two counts."

They leaned forward.

"One of their warriors grew suspicious. I had to deal with him." I slipped out my dagger to show its blood-slicked blade, and pointed at stains on my clothing that even a river had not washed away. "A veteran like us. Can't place exactly where, but I'd seen him before. Probably by our old friend Afrasiab's side. He, on the other hand, recognized me. And that was that."

They made knowing noises.

"The other thing is the main one. That ambitious young upstart, Sohrab, is the size of no Turk I've seen before. A monster. If he's half as good a warrior as they say he is, he will be hell to deal with."

Tus grunted. "I've seen him for myself. Reminded me of another two-legged monster I know. I'll be surprised if he can't fight as well, but really all that either of you need do with the rest of us is lean on us."

I shook my head ruefully. "The monster on your side is slipping. I would not have been discovered so easily, back then. Nevertheless, I have a feeling he and I will soon be leaning on each other. The senior Turk I had to slay seemed to be his close advisor. When he's discovered, I think there will be two of us who aren't happy."

"That may be for the best," Gaev urged. "You can handle him. And that will demoralize the Turks."

This time I nodded. "Let's hope for that. But for the first time in my life, I see a real chance I won't prevail. And that would demoralize *our* ranks." I paused to think. "That's if they know it's the legendary Rostam who's slain. But as yet, no one here but you know who I am. Let's keep it that way for now. Then if I fall, you can say I was just a hired sword."

"That day will never come," Gaev said.

But we all knew it could.

Chapter 7
Sohrab Issues a Challenge

A BLEAK, GRAY DAWN AUGURED THE DAY TO COME. As I left my tent, I heard a commotion on the outskirts of camp. Calling to Zhende Razm, I strode toward it. Warriors scattered out of my way like pygmies. Dark clouds rolled above us. Afrasiab's general, Houman, came out of his tent to see what was going on. I waved him along, and he struggled to keep up.

The group ahead of us churned around something on the ground, with Baman crouched over it. Vultures circling above told me what to expect. But not whom. Baman lifted a somber face to us, and on the ground I recognized a beloved face as I'd never seen it before.

"Zhende bey!" I cried.

The blood had drained from him into a crusted brown pool, leaving the face so gray it blended into a beard specked with red.

I dropped to my knees by his side. The utterly still, silent, grimacing mass of flesh was what remained of the man who had taught me to ride, who had taken me to the scrubland on my first hunt, and with whom my mother and I had shared a monthly meal accompanied by rare spells of laughter.

"Triple the number of sentinels." I composed his stiffening body as I spoke. Someone had already closed his eyes. "Assemble a small contingent to carry the general in honor back to Samangan." Then, pushing up to my feet again: "His killer will answer to my sword before the day is done."

RIDING THE TALL GRAY ZHENDE HAD HAND-PICKED for me, I pulled up at the bank of the Zibad. A respectful distance behind, knowing what was to come, my army arrayed itself and waited. The muddy waters before me flowed placidly toward the Oxus as if nothing had happened. At the whiff of river air, my steed snorted. The sun came out from behind clouds. Across the stream and all along the opposite bank I saw our powerful enemy camped. The Iranians do war in style. Great pavilions in Persian blues, greens, reds, and golds, each with its symbolic banner: the house of the elephant, the house of the lion, the house of the wolf, the house of the griffon, the house of the dragon. A part of me that I now knew to be Persian could admire the splendor, even as the warrior in me appraised the endless numbers and the grieving nephew shook with anger.

I thought back to my old plan to find the Persian father I'd never known. Since then I'd lost count of the fathers and sons I had separated forever. And now I'd lost my Turanian uncle, who'd done his best to be a father to me and had warned me against the warpath. As had my mother, whose wounded heart would be doubly pierced by the loss of her dearest cousin. But at the least I would avenge him and deliver her his murderer's head.

"O Persian warriors!" I sent the words thundering across the water, startling my horse into a skittish dance. "No, that does not fit.… O Persian *cowards* who come by night!"

I looked for signs of increased activity, listened for a reaction.

"Come out in daylight. Come out of hiding and look your enemy in the face."

A low buzz now, some bustle. Then a visible and swiftly growing audience.

"What kind of warriors steal into our camp in the dark to slit a brave warrior's throat?"

Discernible figures in splendid uniform, gesturing and conferring.

"How many cowards did it take to hold my general while you slashed his neck?"

And now a parting of the ranks to make way for a towering figure that pushed through and strode up to the river bank. A veteran, by his graying beard, but unlike the others, garbed roughly in animal hides, as if more given to the hunt than the battlefield. A mercenary, then.

"Only me," he called back in a stentorian voice, "and I am no coward. Your astute general discovered me, so there was no other way. I regret that I had to kill him. He had a noble look about him—convey my apologies to his family."

The fury rose up in me like a torrent. "O murderous hunter," I roared, "I *am* his family! That good man raised me. I will not have your facile apology for his *death*. I will have your head!"

The hulking mercenary bowed that outsized head as if dismayed by the news. "It is true," he called out eventually, lifting it again. "No apology can suffice. But now that I know this, I would not want to spill your blood as well. So think carefully before you demand satisfaction."

I sneered at his assumption. "Worry about the spilling of your own blood first. I will redden the Zibad with it before the day ends! I'll teach you the difference between an easy hunt and a fair fight. Do you have a horse?"

He nodded grimly. "I will ready him for battle. There is a crossing point to your left, and open land where we can face each other. Meet me there."

Chapter 8
The Battle of Rostam and Sohrab

THIS TIME, ON RAKSH'S STRONG BACK, I crossed a stream glittering with sun. A lesser horse might have drowned under the armored burden or rolled me off to drown instead. Yet as we emerged onto the opposite bank, I saw that my enemy's no less burdened steed was equally sturdy. Possibly more, by its evident youth, its unmarked and glistening gray coat. My loyal roan had acquired scars over the years, as had his aging rider.

Our gargantuan young enemy was assessing me up close for the first time. "You look more the warrior," he called out. The anger was still there, but a note of curiosity accompanied it. "And a bigger one I have never seen: the hunting must have been good. What do they call you?"

I eyed the plumed Chinese helmet he affected, and my own anger returned. Too bad I'd been compelled to dispatch his father, but here after all was the bloody invader of Iran who'd slaughtered Gazhdaham and his men. It was imperative I do to him what I'd done to his parent. So if he wanted to chitchat, giving Raksh time to recover, I'd humor the young fool.

"A mercenary needs no name. Anonymity travels well from army to army."

"I see. Does Iran pay you well for your sword?"

"My finances are none of your business."

"I'll make it my business, old man: to take you off their payroll. Permanently."

"It *is* my business to give you the sound cuffing you need, bloodthirsty cub."

"Now that's ironic. But to what do you refer?"

I snorted, causing Raksh's ears to prick up. He was ready to go now. I felt the blood race through my veins again, and welcomed it. "The fort's commander and his men—where was the necessity to kill them all?"

He nodded. "Brave warriors. I called on them to surrender, but they refused. Had they not delayed our advance, we would be well into Iran."

The buzzing in my head was so loud now I shouted over it. "I give you the same choice: surrender to the mercy of the shah or to the point of my spear!"

"Neither," he shouted back and couched his long spear as a lance.

I did the same, pressing my heels to Raksh's sides. Then we were thundering toward each other, gravel flying. My every sense sped up. My focus narrowed. To the tip of my spear rocked by turbulent motion, aligning it at his chain-mail covered chest. Then, as he bore down on me, to the wandering point of *his* spear.

I swung my shield to block it off, and both spears juddered off our shields as the horses passed. I wheeled Raksh around and without a pause urged him forward again. The young fool had stopped to gather his horse on the assumption that I would do the same. So I was halfway to him and gaining speed when he pushed his gray toward us. Just before we crossed he yanked his horse's head so hard it stumbled but turned almost broadside, and my spear found only air.

This time we both gathered ourselves before charging again. And again. And again. And every time lightning reflexes and the clang of iron on iron. Sometimes our spears bounced off the shields into chain-mail across our horses' necks, opening a link or two. Mine shivered past his shield once to open a link along his side. But our spearpoints were blunted by now, and we flung the spears only to see them whiz by our evasive targets.

Skin on fire, breathing hard, I drew my sword. Faintly I heard cheers arise on both sides of the stream—my opponent had drawn his too. A hot wind whipped up sand. The sun was above us now, and sweat popped out all over me. Raksh's flanks were so slick I could smell him.

My enemy's voice was a rasp. "You are no common hunter! A murderous spy, yes, but a warrior. An exceptional warrior."

I nodded acknowledgment. "And you are no cub but an agile young wolf. Nonetheless, a bloodthirsty wolf."

"My bloodlust has its reasons. And I suspect yours go beyond a bag of coins. Else why would the demise of Iran's soldiers stir such anger in a mercenary? Come, tell me who you are."

I had no patience for this distraction. "What does it matter? I am the end for you."

Sword aloft, I charged and brought it crashing down on him. But he parried so powerfully it drove my blade back. His blade came hissing at my neck. I blocked it with my shield rather than sword, or I'd have cut my own throat. My simultaneous thrust was fended off just in time but glanced off the shield into his coat of mail, opening a few links. In an instant his sword clanged down on my helmet. My disbelieving eyes saw its hacked-off central horn tumble through the air, and then the rest of the world span. Our circling horses magnified the effect. I felt myself start to slump off Raksh, before he pulled us clear.

Cheers arose from the Turanians. When my head steadied, I saw blood trickling through a tear in Raksh's chain-mail and down his neck. Then I realized that some of the red I saw was blood dripping down my face. My mind still whirled with something new: doubt. I dared not call it fear. But my hand still gripping the scimitar shook, and I could not make it stop. For the first time in a duel I faced the real possibility that I would be the one to die. The genuine confidence of my prediction, built on victory after victory after nothing but victory, now felt like over-confidence. And my powerful young foe was charging, depriving me of time to gather myself.

I dug so urgently into Raksh's sides that he lurched into a gallop. We crossed at a wild clip, swinging our swords with all our immense strength and practiced precision. The blades clashed in a spectacular rain of sparks and shattered! The Turanian giant stared at the jagged remnant in his hands. Before he blinked I span around and swung for his neck. He barely ducked the broken blade—it shaved the jaunty plume off his helmet. Feathers floated lazily toward the river as he reined his gray away from them.

Facing each other again, we tossed the hilts of our swords aside. This time *my* troops were cheering. A scowl narrowed his eyes.

I took the opening. "Did I ruin your fancy hat?"

His voice shook with fury. "Old man, the blow to your head has addled your senses. Which of us is unblemished and which of us bleeds?"

"I will ruin your pretty face by and by," I said grimly, dismounting and hefting my enormous mace with the two hands it took. But I put a quick hand to the side of Raksh's face, knowing it might be goodbye to my old friend. As soon as my opponent swung off his horse, I set my faithful roan loose toward the water.

We approached cautiously, wielding maces no ordinary man can budge. Precision was now difficult yet no longer necessary. Even a glancing hit from those massive iron clubs could cripple an ox—a perfectly placed blow from mine had felled a berserk elephant. So we circled warily, looking for openings and side-stepping those ponderous swings of death. The shields strapped to our left forearms could take only so much battering; they were reserved to ward off swings that came too close.

Even so, the bold engraving around his shield was soon permanently marred and the rim of mine rippled like a serpent. In the increasingly frequent pauses, I began to hear the thud of my heart. My tongue felt as dry as the grit we'd sent up. The blood across my face had caked, but sweat poured down us. I circled so as to subtly position myself between him and the Zibad. And the next time we backed away it paid off.

"You're strong for an old man," he called out, "but now I can hear you breathing. You're tiring. And I don't tire. Count your remaining moments before I bludgeon you to your knees."

I nodded indulgently but saved my breath. "Think that while you can."

And watchful of him, I backed up to the water. When I was a youngster, my burgeoning size compared to others, especially women, had bothered me. So I stopped eating for a while, hoping to slow my growth. It didn't—I had to resume my prodigious intake eventually, and exploded to this ridiculous height and weight. But in that period, as my strength waned I'd learned to keep it up with whole jugs of water. Now I scooped mouthful after mouthful of cool river tonic. Tracking its delicious progress down my gullet to my chest, I felt my strength return.

I'd half expected him to charge while my hands were off the mace. But he placed the heavy ball of his on the ground and leant indolently upon the long handle. "Take your time, old man."

I took him at his word, splashing water on my face. It unstuck the hairs of my beard and dropped, reddened, back into the stream. Raksh followed my lead, dipping his graceful neck to drink. Clouds drifted slowly above us. Our reflections rippled as he nosed into the water. I wanted to just sit there and look on.

Instead I rose and hefted the mace once more. A dark cloud crept across the sun. A hush came over our armies. "Yes, time to teach you that even an old lion will best a young wolf."

"Ah. But I'm a young lion."

"That you are," I muttered grudgingly. A vast shadow fell over us as clouds obscured the sun, cutting off its heat. An involuntary shiver coursed through me.

"What did you say?"

"You're a young fool! This is your last chance: surrender or die."

His answer was to lift his colossal mace and whirl it like a toy. We approached again, across the darkened bank. This time we swung with such ferocity that the ground shook when the maces thudded into it. At times they glanced heavily off each other, sending us staggering amidst a shower of sparks. At times his mace came so close it was like death whistling past. At times we fended off the maces, and our shields took a beating. Then my mace rang the center of his shield, smashing it into him. He stumbled back and I charged him, swinging for his head.

But the huge fellow side-stepped my death blow with the agility of a dancer. And as the heaviness of my swing pulled me off-balance, he swung his deformed shield into my back. I went sprawling into the dirt. Quick as a Persian leopard, he threw himself astride me, pinning me down and drawing his dagger. He raised it to do to me what I'd done to his father, and in that final moment I roared my defiance: "ROSTAM!"

It paralyzed him. The sheer fury of my old war cry seemed to freeze his hand for the instant it took to yank my knife from its sheath and shove it through the torn links at his side. Then I exploded up into him.

Chapter 9
Sohrab Finds His Father

HIS DREADFUL CRY PIERCED ME even as my dagger tore deep, deep, *deep* into him. It was the cry of a mortally wounded creature. The sound pealed eerily across the river, but our hushed armies could not have known from which of the two warriors on the ground it came. A great shadow hung over us like a shroud. He keeled off me with the knife in his side and lay there on his back, a felled tree trunk of a man. Blood began to wind down his side, onto the sand, and toward the river.

My thoughts and feelings were scattered. Gazhdaham and his brave warriors were avenged. And Iran's bloody invaders had lost their fearsome leader. Yet, as my breath evened and the blood pounding my head began to slow, I felt no thrill of victory. The battle could easily have ended with me bleeding to death and the victorious Turanian looking on. I had never fought a more powerful foe, a more dangerous one, a more fearless one. But up close now, his face, still unmarked though distorted by terrible spasms of pain, was remarkably young.

A shredded, halting voice came out of him. "Old lion, something told me you were no mercenary. But the need to avenge my uncle overpowered it."

"Your uncle," I said sadly, moving his fallen dagger out of reach. "I thought you meant he was your father."

Strangely, a weak laugh came out of him.

"I regret having to slay him—and now you, young lion that you are. I'll see that you're returned to your troops with all the honor you deserve."

He grimaced. "You did not slay me, old lion—your name did!"

I frowned. "My name?"

"Yes. Are you not Rostam?"

"I am."

At that, to my horror, the dying man clutched at me and began to weep. "You foolish, foolish man," he cried. "Why did you not tell me when I inquired?"

Confused, I disengaged his hand from my arm. "Only the commanders of my army know. We could not tell the warriors: had you slain me, their morale would have crumbled."

"As will the morale of my brave warriors now," he said. "But you must end the bloodshed. Let both armies return to their lands: I began this war— it should end with me."

"I will put your dying proposal before both sides. Yet I wonder: would you have felt the same, were our situations reversed and your side held the advantage?"

Again he laughed that strange ironic laugh, then broke off in pain. "I'll tell you. But come close so I may see you."

I moved over, still perplexed, and looked into my enemy's handsome but tortured face. In his eyes as they searched *my* face I saw a terrible madness. And from the sorrow in his voice rang a sublime note of wonder. "It would have ended the instant I knew. This was all for you—my father!"

I drew back like a cobra from a mongoose. "What drivel is this? I have no children."

With a wrenching effort he raised himself on his elbow. And the blood seeped faster around the knife. "Will you deny me even as I die? Cruel man, my mother is the Princess Tahmina!"

I started at the sound of that beloved name, and a flood of thoughts swamped my mind. Was it possible? Had we conceived a child in that too short time together, he would still be little more than a stripling. Could this mountain of a young man truly be my— I dared not even think the word.

Seeing my confusion he said bitterly, "No, it is fate that is cruel. My dear uncle, Zhende Razm, who had seen you on the battlefield and in court, would have identified you for me. Yet before that could happen, he too was destined to die by your blade."

A monstrous understanding continued to build in my head. The look of recognition on his general's face, the hazily familiar name. Tahmina had no siblings, but she had spoken of a close cousin. "Did your mother," I ventured before my voice cracked. "Did she tell you…?"

He nodded. "She did better. She gave me your old armband: the seal of Zaul you'd given her for protection. Peel away my chain-mail so you may see it."

My hands shook as I did. And then, eons after I'd made a parting gift of it to the most beautiful woman in the world, there it was: my father's seal glowing demonically through the unnatural darkness, the griffon Simorgh in all her brilliant plumage. It blinded me. My head whirling, I put both hands to the ground to keep myself from collapsing. My helmet tumbled off. When my vision began to clear, I groped my way over conglomerates of dirt toward the dagger.

But a death grip on my wrist stopped me from picking it up. "Before I set out to find you, I swore to her that I would bring you back to Samangan. Now you must keep my promise."

I lifted my matted head at that. "Nothing will stop me. And I will carry you with me in honor. There are potions and elixirs—we will find one."

His smile was painful. "The potion does not exist that can seal this deep wound. When the knife comes out, I will go fast. But first, remove my helmet. Let us not be soldiers. Let us finally be father and son."

I lifted his helmet. Hair as black as the night fell across an uncreased forehead, and I began to weep. "My son!" I cried out, and bowed my head in anguish.

His voice was filled with wonder. "I have waited all my life to hear those words. Will you say them once more?"

"My son, my son, my son…" I could not stop saying it.

A deep sigh came out of him, and the voice grew frail. "Now I may go."

He reached around to grip the knife. His face contorted, and with a final burst of immeasurable strength, he drew the knife from its deadly sheath. The lifeblood poured from the open wound. It swelled the red tributary that wound slowly across the sand, until it dripped into the Zibad. The stream carried it past our murmuring camps, as clouds rolled and fog arose, then on toward the Oxus. The great river flowed as if unaware of blood in the waters. And at last it spilled into the Aral Sea.

The Singer, III

AND SO AN UNEASY TRUCE CAME TO PASS between Iran and Turan. But the day came when Rostam overthrew Afrasiab and made Persia one under Kai Kusru, may Ohrmuzd smile upon him. He will live to a good age and be loved by his people. Still one day he will step down from the throne to embark on a pilgrimage into the snowy Alborz Mountains, where the ancient griffons fly. His successors will make Persia an empire that covers the earth. Yet one day that empire too will crumble. The days of shahs and princes will end. The power of the land will pass into the hands of every common man and woman. People like us will inherit the world.

And now the fire sinks low. My song of warriors and princes and princesses must also end. But it shall be sung across the land forever. The day will come when I need not be there to sing it. You will hear my voice as if I were. The day will come when you shall see it unfold around you, as if Tahmina were here in her radiant beauty and the colossus Rostam there to kiss her. The ground will quake beneath you as Raksh and the gray stallion thunder toward each other and Sohrab's scimitar rings on Rostam's shield. Sohrab will live again. And die again. The world will weep for the father who unknowingly slew his son.

Has the fire, too, died? Go, then, to your flock and your home. But return tomorrow, and I will sing for you the song of Simorgh the giant griffon who raised Zaul the white-haired infant who wooed Rudabeh the princess of Kabul who bore Rostam the hero of Persia who…

Afterword & Acknowledgments

In 1990, when I was still a systems programmer-analyst about a year before returning to school for an M.A. in English & Creative Writing, a young woman I'd met who was self-conscious of her ethnicity told me she hadn't been able to stop crying for three days after her first breakup. I'm sure she meant she cried repeatedly every time she thought of it, but I had a vision of her crying when eating, crying when speaking, crying when sleeping, literally crying nonstop for three days. So I wrote a Wildean fairytale called "The Plain Fairy," later renamed "A Coming," in which three days became three decades. But the rest of my writing was in the school of realism, so when it was time to select stories, new and old, for my creative-writing thesis in 1993, my committee chairperson Dr. Kathy Hassall rightly said it should be unified around realism. I put "A Coming" aside and continued to read and write realism, through the publications of my eventually book-length 2001 collection and my 2016 novel.

While I was writing the latter, however, someone recommended Aimee Bender's fantastic (in both senses of the word) collection, *The Girl in the Flammable Skirt*. Inspired, I wrote a Kafkaesque/Ovidian story that pushed past the bounds of realism: "Steven." A Calvinoesque alternate-world story, "The Straight," would follow. I was also still writing realism, sometimes experimenting with form, as in "All Right, Now, Cupid," the online profile questions/subtitles in which are straight off the OkCupid web site. And the hybrid form of "Family Tree": when my aunt Sheroo Fracis was in hospital with terminal cancer, my cousin Xerxes Fracis took a beautiful photograph of his children—her grandchildren—and me, all sitting on the low-lying branches of a tree. It struck me as a literal image of the common metaphor. So though all the stories reflected an underlying authorial sensibility, they seemed irreconcilably divided along the realism/fantasy line. That is until a friend who'd been the partial basis for a composite character in my earlier work said I ought to write "true fiction." That paradoxical phrase, I realized, could cover all varieties of stories. (I should add that the friend is not at all a basis for the character Arun's questionable side. So credit for the original phrase and that eventually helpful advice goes to that friend, but it's still best he remain unnamed. I've had some readers of other narratives jump to wrong conclusions, and I don't want that to happen to him.) So once I wrote a story with that title, I saw that a new collection could now be unified under *True Fiction*.

When it was time to write a concluding story, I finally—thirty years after

I'd started to write—circled around to the ancient one I'd arguably been named to retell/rewrite/re-envision/rework/renew. My mother, Dinsi Fracis, had often told me of my great-grandfather Sohrab Bharucha, whose favorite grandchild she'd been. Even before I was born, she and my father, Homi Fracis, decided that a male child would be named Sohrab. So in fact I was not directly named for the legendary Persian-Turkish warrior. But naturally I did become familiar with the tragic story and the spectacular ancient epic of which it was part. Its millennia-old, originally orally portrayed father-son dynamic had found resonance in such pairs as Oedipus and Laius all the way through to Luke Skywalker and Darth Vader. Yet when I moved to the West, I found that, like many things in my past, even its existence was hardly known here. And once I learned the modern craft of creative writing, I often felt the story would benefit from the application of that craft. Translations of the episode within Ferdowsi's immense and sprawling Persian epic, *Shahnameh*, suffered from too much reportage and summary instead of scenes with dialogue etc.. And while Matthew Arnold focused on the battle scene, vivid and heroic in spite of summarized reportage of the consequently much-needed context, the narrative felt bogged down by its ornate density. Fine for the magnificent 19th Century narrative poem that it is, but I wanted the full essential story rendered in scenes to move along for greater readability. Finally, the point of view in all the past narratives was a distancing third-person, from the outside in, whereas I felt the various psychological motivations and internal conflicts could be explored and rendered most deeply through direct first-person points of view, i.e. from the inside out. Those multiple first-person voices, as well as the dialogue, organically became more conversational/contemporary, another update that boosted the story's readability.

In addition to those mentioned above, I'd like to thank the editors of anthologies and magazines that published some of the stories. Shane Hinton and Ryan Rivas solicited and selected "All Right, Now, Cupid" for Burrow Press's *We Can't Help It If We're From Florida*. Shane, the anthology's guest-editor, had some nice edits that I incorporated. Caleb Sarvis and Jared Rypkema solicited and selected "Open Mic" for Bridge Eight Press's *15 Views of Jacksonville*. The working title while I was drafting it, "Coffee Talk," had organically morphed into "Open Mic," which made it a natural choice to open the anthology as well as this collection. And Caleb, Bridge Eight's fiction editor at the time, kept his edits to a couple of nice ones. (I should add that Katie Flynn green-lighted the chorus of her original song as it's represented in the story. She reminded me that it was actually "I hate those boys," but said I should leave it the way I'd misremembered it. The other chorus, too, is quoted from an original song—by an unknown amateur musician as described and fuzzily attributed in the same passage.) My thanks to April Gray Wilder and Mark Ari, who solicited and selected "True Fiction" for *Flock*. April, the editor-in-chief, and the copy editor Sarah Cotchaleovich had several nice edits. And April and Ari invited me to read and speak on *Flock*'s 15th Anniversary panel at the 2018 AWP Conference in Tampa. The editors of Z Publishing House solicited and selected "A Coming" for *America's Emerging Science Fiction and Fantasy Writers*. Their edition gave the speech of my non-gendered godhead/pronoun Xe its italics. Thanks to Yeow Kai Chai, fiction editor at *Quarterly Literary Review Singapore*, for publishing "Steven." Thanks to Kaartikeya Bajpai, editor of *The Bombay Review*, for publishing "The Straight." Thanks also to Alexis Williams and Don Williams for selecting "Steven" as a finalist for *New Millennium Writings*. In addition to Stephen Jay Gould's essay, "Sex and Size," Steve Jones's book, *Y: The Descent of Men*, was a useful resource when writing "Steven." I'd also like to thank C.C. (Charlie) Finlay of *Fantasy & Science Fiction* for his helpful feedback on a first draft of "The Straight." And Doug Henning, reading the Zoroastrian Gathas with the help of an Avestan (Old Persian) glossary, kindly added the aspect of water to my understanding of my own name's etymology. I then adjusted, in "The Legend of Rostam and Sohrab," the two heroes' interpretations of the name, which now foreshadow blood in the Oxus. Many thanks to Bridge Eight Press's editors for selecting *True Fiction* as a national finalist for the Bridge Eight Press Fiction Prize. And to Minerva Rising Press for selecting *True Fiction* as a national finalist for the Rosemary Daniell Fiction Prize. A big thanks to Dzanc Books editor-in-chief, Michelle Dotter, for selecting *True Fiction* as a national finalist for the Dzanc Books Story Collection Prize.

That brings me to my wonderful press director, Kimberly (Kim) Verhines, and editorial assistant *par excellence*, Katherine (Katt) Noble, at Stephen F. Austin University Press. I can't thank you enough for selecting *True Fiction*, for believing in it so strongly, for making such a lovely book, and for bringing it to your readers. May there be many. Finally I'd like to thank all the readers—including friends, family, teaching colleagues, scholars, and fellow writers—who over the years were so kind as to let me know how much they'd liked, even loved, my books. It kept me writing.

SOHRAB HOMI FRACIS is the first Asian American to win the Iowa Short Fiction Award, for his debut collection, *Ticket to Minto: Stories of India and America*. Publishers Weekly called it "A reminder of how satisfying the short story form can be...the work of an impressive new talent." India Currents pronounced it "Stunning in its breadth and scope of language and description." It was translated into German and also released in India. His novel, *Go Home*, was shortlisted worldwide by Stanford University Libraries for the William Saroyan International Prize. Folio Weekly called it "a quest tale of the highest order.... Fracis is both a deft realist and master mesmerist." Singapore Poetry described it as "newly poignant and even heartbreaking." Fracis taught literature and creative writing at University of North Florida. He was Twin Cities Visiting Writer in Residence at Augsburg University, and Artist in Residence at Yaddo. The South Asian Literary Association bestowed on him its Distinguished Achievement Award.